M 6

W9-AKT-127

FP?

Alexis

and the
missing
ingredient

This book is a work of fiction. Any references to historical events, real people, or real places are used fictitiously. Other names, characters, places, and events are products of the author's imagination, and any resemblance to actual events or places or persons, living or dead, is entirely coincidental.

SIMON SPOTLIGHT

An imprint of Simon & Schuster Children's Publishing Division

1230 Avenue of the Americas, New York, New York 10020

Copyright © 2013 by Simon & Schuster, Inc.

All rights reserved, including the right of reproduction in whole or in part in any form.

SIMON SPOTLIGHT and colophon are registered

trademarks of Simon & Schuster, Inc.

Text by Elizabeth Doyle Carey

Chapter header illustrations by Emmy Reis

Designed by Laura Roode

For information about special discounts for bulk purchases, please contact

Simon & Schuster Special Sales

at 1-866-506-1949 or business@simonandschuster.com.

Manufactured in the United States of America 0913 FFG

First Edition 2 4 6 8 10 9 7 5 3 1

ISBN 978-1-4424-8587-7 (pbk)

ISBN 978-1-4424-8588-4 (hc)

ISBN 978-1-4424-8589-1 (eBook)

Library of Congress Catalog Card Number 2013946717

Alexis

and the

missing

ingredient

by coco simon

Simon Spotlight

New York   London   Toronto   Sydney   New Delhi

CHAPTER I

The Best-Laid Plans

$\mathcal{M}$ost people would be thrilled to have off a couple of random days from school in the middle of the term, but me—not so much. I hate to lose momentum. I also dislike it when my schedule is disrupted. I know it sounds nuts, but I'm the kid who listens to the radio on snow days hoping they *don't* say my school's name.

So all this is why I was just a little bit bummed out that it was Teacher Development Week at my school, and we'd have off Thursday and Friday. I know, I know, it's crazy, but like I said, I'm a creature of habit and I like structure.

I also do not really like making social plans. I am happy to go to most things that other people plan, but thinking up activities and getting everyone on board isn't my favorite thing to do. Don't get me wrong; I love planning most everything else. I plan almost all our budgets and projects, but something like what we're going to do on a Saturday afternoon . . . not so much. I leave that to my friends in the Cupcake Club: Emma, Mia, and Katie. In fact, I mostly just count on Emma, who has been my best friend since we were little. We like to do the same stuff, and I always include her if I want to do something, like go to the movies, and vice versa. Somehow it just always works out that there's something to do.

Mia, on the other hand, is great at coming up with fun ideas, like, "Hey, let's all go to the mall and get our nails painted neon" or "Let's go to the department store and try on one of every kind of accessory" or "Let's do a time capsule!" Katie, too, comes up with clever plans, like making a gingerbread mansion or building a haunted house for Emma's little brother and his friends. I do admit I had a fun plan one year, when I convinced us all to go to the homecoming parade and game in costumes—with boys!—but that was an exception since it came from my desperate need to spend time with my crush, Matt Taylor.

So now I'm faced with four empty days in a

row and no plans, and Emma has the nerve to be going away!

Sure, she gave me plenty of advance warning, but her saying she's going camping with her family and my realizing I need to dream up some plans were not connected in my mind until the last minute. (For me, the last minute means the weekend before.)

Emma and I were lying on the floor in my room, watching cute animals on YouTube, and she was counting out the reasons on her fingers of why she was dreading camping.

"Bugs, cold, uncomfortable, no bathrooms, bad food . . ."

"No me!"

"Right! No you, only boys except my parents . . ." Emma has three brothers. That's a lot of brothers.

"Wait! When are you gone from?" I asked.

Emma sighed. "We leave Wednesday, right after school. In fact, *from* school, I think. And then we don't get back until Sunday morning!"

"OMG. Four nights. That is long. And meanwhile, I'll be— Wait! What will I be doing?" I'd suddenly realized I had ignored my number-one motto (Failing to plan is planning to fail) and had not made one plan for the weekend. I sat upright in shock. "So, wait. Wednesday night, I'll . . . do homework. Thursday *day* I can . . . do a little more, like, extra-credit homework and tie up any loose ends with Cupcake Club business. Maybe work on my speech for the Future Business Leaders of America summit." I relaxed a little, realizing I could fill the days with getting ahead on my work. I took a deep breath. "But Thursday night, Friday? *Friday* night? Saturday and *Saturday night*? Oh no. That's a lot of time to fill!" I twirled my hair nervously. "What should I do?"

Emma looked at me. "You are so lucky. I'd kill to be doing nothing." She sighed.

"So stay! You can totally stay with me!" I started to relax again immediately, imagining the luxury of having a built-in best friend for four days. I grinned. "There's so much fun stuff we could do. I'm sure you'd have lots of great ideas!"

Emma sighed again heavily. "I can't. It's required. My mom thinks it might be our last camping trip as a family before Sam goes away to school."

My heart sank. "Humph!" I said.

"Maybe you and Dylan could do something?" she asked helpfully. "Go somewhere?" She shrugged.

I scowled. "Going anywhere with Dylan is not

4

exactly a laugh a minute," I said. Though my older sister can be nice sometimes, mostly she doesn't want me around, and isn't afraid to show it or let me know it. "Even if she would do anything with me," I added.

"What about your grandparents'?"

"Wow. Wait a minute! *That* is not a bad idea! Even for a night that might be fun. I'll ask my mom to ask them." My grandparents live about an hour away in a rambling old farmhouse that's filled with cool stuff, and they have lots of land and a trampoline and a barn and everything. That could be good. I felt a tiny bit better just thinking of it.

Emma thought again. "Maybe Dylan would take you to the city?" she suggested, then we both laughed. If Dylan was going to the city, it certainly wouldn't be with me. "Okay, okay. Just brainstorming."

"Hey! Speaking of brainstorming, we've got to resolve that PTA meeting menu."

"Oh boy." Emma closed her eyes and put her head in her hands.

We'd had one of our rare Cupcake Club blowups the day before, just talking about what we should bake for the PTA meeting we were hired to cater in two weeks.

Our business, the Cupcake Club, bakes and sells custom cupcakes for all kinds of events. Along with Mia and Katie, Emma and I have built a pretty good business of baking, with regular clients and signature recipes and great reviews on our website. PTA meetings and things like that are good venues for us, because there are lots of local parents all in one place, so we get to wow them with our skills and hopefully get new business out of some of them. It's a great way to earn some money and it's a ton of fun, too.

I am the business-minded brain of the group—the CEO. I plan our schedules, do the purchasing and manage the inventory, work out pricing—stuff like that. I realize it's funny that I am great at plans and schedules for work and for school, but terrible at it socially. It's just the way I am. My mom always says, You can't be great at everything, so be great at the most important things. That's what I try to do.

Anyway, during our meeting yesterday, all four of us had different ideas. Some of us wanted to go plain and basic, others wanted to really go wild and show what we were capable of. Two of us felt it was all about how great the cupcakes would look, while one said it was all about how they would taste, and the fourth member couldn't decide which was more important.

"All I know is, we need something really great because it's an ideal marketing opportunity for us. All those parents in one place ... Those are our customers! Think of the birthday parties they organize, never mind book clubs and baby showers!" I said now to Emma.

Emma agreed. "I know, I know. I don't know why that turned into such a big fight. Mia and Katie were pretty irate."

"Well, they did seem better today, but that's probably because none of us brought it up."

Emma nodded. "We'll need to figure it out soon."

"A stitch in time saves nine," I agreed soberly.

Later, when Emma was leaving, she said, "Hey, don't forget Mia and Katie are around next weekend ... at least for part of it. They'll have something fun going on for sure. Call them!"

"Right," I said. "Will do." But, in fact, I probably wouldn't. Even though I spend a lot of time with Mia and Katie, it's kind of like our foursome is a combination of two pairs: Mia and Katie are one, and Emma and I are the other. All together, the four of us are a great group, and two by two, we are good pairs. But I have never really hung out with just Mia or just Katie, and I don't really ever hang out with them without Emma. It's just the way it works out. I would almost be kind of nervous to hang out with them without Emma. I know it sounds nuts, but that's just how I feel. Anyway, I still had weird feelings about them since the PTA fight. I figured I'd be laying low for a while.

As soon as I shut the door after Emma, I called up to my mom, "Mom! Can you call Grandma to see if I can go stay with her this week?"

Then I ran to my desk and sent out an e-mail asking the Cupcakers to meet next Sunday to brainstorm some ideas for the PTA meeting. It was chicken of me to do it via e-mail and to put it off for another week, but whatever. At least it was being addressed. Phew.

Anyway, that's how it came to be Thursday morning and how I was putting my toothbrush into my already-packed overnight bag to go to my grandma's house. My granddad Jim was picking me up at nine, and I was really looking forward to my two nights at their house. (Jim is actually my stepgranddad, but he's the only one I've ever known.) Tonight we would have a feast and watch scary movies and eat popcorn and my grandma's caramel brownies. Tomorrow we're going to go on a long hike around the property and then to see the new kittens in the barn and lots of other fun stuff. My grandma is a great cook, and she isn't stingy with the butter or sugar the way my health-nut mom is. I knew I'd be eating well and sleeping well and getting lots of personal attention at the farmhouse, since Dylan was staying home so that she could go to the city with friends for the day. (She always has major plans, way in advance.) It was going to be great.

I heard the phone ring as I started down the stairs and kind of absentmindedly noticed it was a little early for the phone to ring. When I got to the kitchen, my mom was speaking urgently and had one hand gripping the countertop so hard, her knuckles were white.

My mom spoke anxiously into the phone. "Is she going to be okay? What did the doctor say it was?" She looked at me but didn't really register my presence. I dropped my bag to the floor. Who was she talking about?

"How long are they keeping her?"

Pause.

"Can we come out and help you?"

Dylan walked in and stood next to me, and we watched our mom talk on the phone.

Who? mouthed Dylan.

My mom stared blankly at us.

"Okay, well, please call me as soon as she comes back and I can drive out there later this morning. Thanks so much, Jim. Give her a huge hug from all of us."

Dylan and I looked at each other in shock. Grandma?

My mom hung up the phone and sat heavily at the kitchen table.

"Mom?" I asked quietly.

She looked up, and her eyes were teary. "It's fine. It just caught me off guard. Sorry. It's Grandma but they think she's going to be okay. She fell down the last step to the basement and bumped her head, so they took her to the hospital to make sure she was okay."

"Oh!" My hand flew to my mouth.

My mom smiled. "Well, you know Grandma can be a little clumsy. Jim said it could have been a lot worse, and she's in very good hands. They really think she's going to be fine. They're keeping her at the hospital for observation, just to be safe. She'll need to rest and take it easy for a few days."

"That's scary, Mom," said Dylan, reaching over to rub my mom's back. I wished I'd thought of that.

"Poor Grandma!" I said. "You're going to see her later?"

My mom nodded. "Jim said I didn't need to come, but I hate to think of him out there at the hospital all alone. I'll go into work for a bit this morning, then head straight out and probably spend the night at the house. And you girls can— Oh, Lexi! I just realized! It was your special trip today. I'm so sorry, honey!" She got up to give me a hug.

"That's okay," I said into her shoulder. "Do you want me to come with you to the hospital, anyway?"

She let go and smoothed back my hair. "No, but thank you. I think I'd better go alone. Maybe Dad could take you girls out for a treat tonight, since you're missing your trip, Lexi."

I nodded. "Okay. And maybe we could watch a movie."

"Sure," she said. She picked up her cell phone to look at her day's schedule and then she called my dad to tell him the new plan.

Dylan and I looked at each other. "Well . . . ," she said.

"I'm going to just do my homework today," I said.

I could see her relief. "Okay, are you sure?" Dylan asked. She stared at me for a moment, making sure I wasn't really upset.

"Totally," I said. Nobody wants to go where they're not welcome.

"Okay."

And that was that.

CHAPTER 2

Mall Brats

A day is kind of a long time to fill all by yourself, and, really, a person can only do so much work before they have to go watch reruns of *Celebrity Ballroom*.

Here's what I did: I made note cards for Latin; I did all my math homework for the upcoming week; I wrote the first draft of an English essay I have due next week; I studied for my history quiz; and I balanced the books for the Cupcake Club, updated our website, and sent out some e-bills to a few late-paying clients. My room was already very clean and my school stuff was organized, so I didn't need to do any of that.

After all that it was only eleven forty-five in the morning.

I watched TV for a good hour, forcing myself to relax and to enjoy the downtime. Then I had a P-B-and-J sandwich, folded the laundry, and went online, and by then it was only one thirty.

It occurred to me I could call Mia and Katie to see what they were doing. I knew they were planning to go to the city to stay with Mia's dad at some point, but I felt like a bad friend because I hadn't really made a mental note of when they'd actually be going. I'd feel like a loser if I reached out to them and they were already there and I was busted for not remembering their plans. Plus, there was a little of the PTA fight awkwardness still out there. I decided not to call them.

My mom called to check in, and I practically lunged for the phone, trying to keep the disappointment out of my voice when I heard it was her, even though I didn't really expect Mia or Katie to call me. The good news was Grandma was going to be fine. My mom said my grandparents couldn't stop talking about how badly they felt that they'd let me down and how they would have to make it up to me. I smiled, looking forward to that, but obviously not feeling sorry for myself compared to the situation my grandma was in. I didn't have the nerve to tell my mom how bored I was, and I didn't want to burden her any more than she already was, anyway. I told her I was fine, and she seemed happy with that answer and told me to have fun tonight with my dad.

My dad called to say he'd be home by five, so I should pick a movie and find the showtime and then decide where I wanted to go to dinner and if I wanted to eat before or after the movie. This is the kind of planning I hate to do, but with all this time on my hands, I did it just to fill the day. (Argh! It was only one forty-five.)

I do have other friends from school, like from my classes and Future Business Leaders of America, and also some friends from summer camp who might be around, but no one I would just cold-call to hang out. I thought about it a bit. It was weird, I guess. I did everything with Emma. I wondered if this was normal.

Sitting around listening to the kitchen clock tick, I thought about how my mom always told us only boring people get bored. I don't really think that's fair to say, especially if you live in the suburbs. There just isn't much to do, especially if you're a kid on your own. I got out my bike and went for a ride around my neighborhood, and I didn't see a soul. I was a little scared to go much farther by myself, so I kind of circled the same blocks a few times, then went back home. I usually think the girls who are always dreaming up social stuff for the weekends are silly—after all, there's always work that could be done, isn't there?—but I was starting to see I'd really just been lazy all these years, letting my friends come up with plans or letting my teachers' assignments fill my days.

Humph.

For a little while after I got home, I worked on my life lists. These are the lists I keep in my planner, things like places I'd like to visit, cupcake recipe ideas, things to do in New York City, and wardrobe staples to find. My lists were pretty up-to-date, though, so I quickly grew tired of them.

By four o'clock I was dressed for my night out with my dad, sitting on the sofa, clicking through channels on the TV. And then an awful thought hit me: Today was bad, but what about tomorrow? *And the day after that?* What was I going to do to fill all this time? I really missed Emma, and not just because I was lazy.

I looked at the phone. Should I call Katie or Mia? I felt nervous thinking about it, which I knew was silly. But what were they doing right now? Weren't they already in the city? Maybe I could call, and if no one picked up, they'd never know. I wouldn't leave a message. But if they did pick up, well . . . maybe they'd want to come to the movies or do something in the morning if they weren't going to the city then.

So who to call first? Mia was a tiny bit intimidating, I had to admit. She's stylish, she grew up in the city for most of her life, she has lots of other friends there. . . .

So . . . Katie! I knew her number by heart, which is kind of weird, because I don't really call her that much. I reached out for the receiver, then shied away from it, tapping my chin with my finger instead. Should I? What would I say if she was there? *Oh, hey, my trip got canceled and I'm done with every scrap of homework, so what are you up to?*

That wouldn't be so bad, would it?

I reached for the phone again, and then I heard the front door open. "Hello! Anyone home?"

"Dadddyyyy!" I jumped up and ran to hug him.

"Whoa, tiger!" He laughed. "How did I get so lucky to deserve a greeting like this?"

"I'm just happy to see you!" I declared. He didn't know I'd have been happy to see any other living, breathing soul at that point, but I wasn't about to put it to him that way.

He changed, and we went to the mall, where we had an early dinner at Spatinis (yum!) and saw a seven o'clock showing of the newest James Bond movie, which was really good. When we got home at around ten, Dylan was already there with one of her best friends, Meredith, who was sleeping over, and they kind of let me be in the same room as them for an hour or so before I went to bed. That was a thrilling social interaction, let me tell you. It mostly consisted of the two of them Facebooking and IM'ing on Dylan's computer while alternately shushing each other and giving me meaningful looks. What*ever*. Like I cared or had any idea who they were talking about. I finally went to my room, and I don't think they even noticed I had left.

In the morning, my dad came in to say good-bye before he left for work. He told me he had asked Dylan last night if she'd keep an eye on me during the day today and that he or my mom would check in soon to see what our plans were. I rolled over and decided to go back to sleep for a few minutes. When I next woke up, it was already nine thirty, which is like sleeping half the day away!

I jumped out of bed and went into the hall just as Dylan opened her door, fully dressed and followed closely by Meredith. Dylan stopped dead in her tracks when she saw me.

"Uh-oh," she said.

"What?" asked Meredith.

"What?" I echoed, looking down at my pj's. Was it something I was wearing? I felt my hair. Did I have bed head?

Dylan frowned. "I forgot that I told my dad I'd babysit Lexi today. Ugh!"

"'Babysit'?" I said scornfully. "Seriously?"

"Well, 'include' was the word he used, I think. Hmm. This changes things."

"I don't know what it changes for you, but I've got to use the bathroom and brush my teeth, so I will see you downstairs," I huffed. As if I was going to stand there and listen to those two discuss how I'd ruined their plans for the day.

I got dressed and made my way to the kitchen, sure that I'd find a note like, "Hey, had to dash. Will check in later!," but they were actually sitting there in their jackets. Dylan surveyed my outfit critically.

"What?" I asked, pouring myself a bowl of some sawdusty health cereal my mom buys.

"Just . . . you really can't wear that."

I looked down. Jeans, T-shirt, sneakers. "Why?" I didn't see anything wrong with it.

Dylan looked at Meredith and rolled her eyes. "Because you need to look a little more stylish if you're going to hang out with us. It can't look like we have my little sister along for the day."

"But you do!" I protested.

"But I might *not*, if you don't cooperate!" snarled Dylan.

I took a huge bite of my cereal and chomped loudly, getting out all my aggression on those little bran pods.

"Listen, we are going to the mall to meet . . . well, maybe to meet . . . this cute guy who works at Sneakerocity."

I swallowed. "A shoe salesman?"

"Very funny—not. It's the new skateboarding store in the mall, and a guy from one of my classes works there. Mike Turnbull. And we are going to very casually be available for lunch with him on his break—if we time it right. Therefore, we cannot look like we are hauling around a kid with us."

"Why are you leaving now?" I asked, looking at the clock. It was a quarter to ten.

Dylan and Meredith rolled their eyes at each other. "Because we don't know what time he gets off for lunch. We need to be available at any possible time."

"We've been planning this for weeks," added Meredith.

I put down my spoon and sighed. The day loomed ahead of me, long and empty. No more homework, no more Cupcake business to attend to. Just me and the ballroom dance reruns. I sighed again.

"What do I have to wear?"

We took a taxi to the mall, and it was ten thirty by the time we were inside and scoping out Sneakerocity from a hidden perch inside Soapy Chic, which is a fancy soap and bath store, where no boy would ever tread. I was uncomfortable in an itchy funnel-neck sweater of Dylan's and some skinny jeans that were so cropped, I looked like Pippi Longstocking. Dylan and Meredith had assured me I looked "good enough" (thanks a lot), so I was allowed to be with them rather than left on my own at Homeschooling, where I like to play with the colorful math manipulatives.

I moved around Soapy Chic, sniffing bath salts and sampling hand lotions. I felt that if we were going to use their store as a launching pad, we could at least pay some sort of rent by buying one little item or another.

A saleslady materialized at my side. "Hello, dear. Is there anything I can help you with today?"

I smiled. "I'm just looking, so far. Thanks."

She smiled kindly. "Okay. I know one thing I can point out is our sample area, where we have trial sizes of all our bestselling products. They make great party favors and are lots of fun to bring on sleepovers—a different one for each girl, so everyone can try them!" She pointed toward the area and then moved across the store to straighten some marginally unaligned body creams.

Sleepovers. Party favors. I missed my friends.

I selected four different little hand creams, each $1.99, and put them on the counter.

Suddenly, Dylan called to me, "Alexis! Move out! Now! He's on the loose!"

My heart leaped in my chest, like I was on a real spy mission, but I still needed to pay. Oh, and I didn't give a darn. There was that, too.

"I'll . . . I'll catch up!" I replied.

"Your loss!" Dylan rolled her eyes at me and dashed out of the store with Meredith.

"I'm sure . . . ," I muttered.

The saleslady wrapped each lotion beautifully and really took her time, which was fine with me, since I had nothing else to do. We talked about how they merchandise—which is how they display the items—and price reductions, and I learned quite a bit. That kind of info will be handy if the Cupcake Club ever opens a retail store, which is one of my little dreams. Finally, I took my bag and left, promising to visit Nancy, the nice saleslady, soon.

Back out in the mall, I swung my bag and window-shopped, knowing I had Meredith and Dylan to fall back on if I got lonely but not feeling like I urgently needed to find them yet. Mom never really let me walk around the mall by myself . . . well, ever. *Huh,* I thought. Then I found myself outside my favorite store, Big Blue, and as I put my hand on the door to open the big blue double doors, I saw something at the back of the store that caught my eye. It was Mia and Katie!

Relief and happiness flooded me, but then I suddenly felt shy and also a tiny bit mad. Like, why didn't they call me to go to the mall? Of course, I was supposed to be at my grandparents', but still. Then I remembered our PTA cupcake fight, and I got even more shy. I hesitated, even contemplated turning around to flee. But then Katie turned and caught sight of me, and there was no escape.

CHAPTER 3

All Aboard!

"Alexis?" Katie cried.

"What are you doing here?" Mia called, then added, "Great outfit!" (Mia worships Dylan's fashion sense, so this wasn't a surprise comment.)

I took a deep breath and smiled as I walked toward them. "Hey, guys!"

"We thought you were at your grandparents'," said Katie, a look of confusion on her face.

"Oh. Yeah. Well, it got canceled. My grandma is in the hospital, so the visit was postponed."

"Wait, *what?* Is she okay?" Mia asked, very concerned.

"You should have told us! That's terrible," said Katie. "What's going to happen? And how's your granddad?"

I filled them in, having forgotten that they'd met my grandparents on a few occasions. Their concern was really touching, and I was surprised they were annoyed I hadn't told them. But then the worst part came.

"So, wait, you've *been here* the past two days?" asked Mia.

"Well . . . yeah. I mean, I didn't have anywhere else to go." I shrugged and looked away.

Katie frowned. "So what have you been doing?"

I now felt uncomfortable. I cleared my throat. "Uh . . . well. I've been doing homework and Cupcake Club business . . . ," I offered lamely.

Mia was looking at me carefully. "The whole time?"

"Why didn't you call us?" asked Katie in a quiet voice.

I tried to make light of it. "I was embarrassed I couldn't remember when you guys were going to the city. I'm such a knucklehead!" I thumped myself on the skull to illustrate my point. I wasn't about to mention anything about the PTA cupcake war, either.

Mia and Katie exchanged a quick glance. I gulped and looked away.

"Wow," said Mia. "I think we should be hurt."

"Right?" agreed Katie. "We thought we were your best friends!"

"You are!" I said in a rush. "I'm sorry! I just . . . I felt like a loser, and I really couldn't remember your exact plans, so, like I said . . ."

Katie and Mia exchanged a questioning look that I thought was like, *Should we let her off the hook?* But it turned out that wasn't what they were silently asking each other, because they both seemed to reach the same decision and turned back to me with smiles.

"So you'll come to the city with us, then," said Mia definitively.

Katie nodded. "Totally!"

I could feel a blush pinken my face. "Oh . . . I . . . but . . ."

"No. It's decided. You have absolutely no say in the matter," said Mia, folding her arms across her chest.

I felt a swirl of emotions inside. If I had been a cupcake right then, I would have been tie-dye flavored—all mixed up. I wanted to go to the city, of course, but I didn't want to intrude, and I felt like a third wheel. And I was honestly a touch annoyed at not being invited in the first place. On the other hand, I had absolutely no plans, and I was dreading the rest of the weekend alone. I knew it would be a relief to my parents if I had something fun to do. I took a deep breath. "Okay! I'll come! Thanks!"

I borrowed Mia's cell phone to call my mom for permission, and my mom was so happy for me, it seemed I'd made the right decision. After I hung up, Mia and Katie hugged me and squealed, then the three of us jumped up and down a little, and I *knew* I'd made the right decision.

"Okay, we're getting on a one o'clock train," Mia said.

"And we're bringing lunch on the train, so what can we get for you?" Katie asked.

"And make sure you pack . . ."

"But, wait, don't forget . . ."

And Mia and Katie filled me in on all their fun plans while we set out to find Dylan and Meredith to let them know I'd had a much better offer than stalking boys with them at the mall all day.

As we walked, Mia called her dad to tell him the news, and I held my breath while I listened to her side of the conversation. I was waiting to hear any inkling of my presence being a hassle, because I would have quickly canceled. But it seemed like he was perfectly happy to have me.

My mom called back on Mia's phone to say

my dad would meet me outside the mall in fifteen minutes to bring me home to pack and then to the train station. She said she'd call Dylan to let her know, so I didn't have to keep searching the massive mall for her (a task that would have happily killed an hour for me, back before I'd had this new plan), and she reminded me, with a certain tone, that I wasn't supposed to be walking around the mall by myself in the first place. "But—" I started, and she cut me off with, "I will definitely talk to your sister about this." Wow, Dylan was totally going to get blamed for this. Somehow this didn't upset me.

Mia e-mailed me a quick list of what I'd need to pack, and then we split up, so they could go meet Mia's mom for a ride home and I could go meet my dad.

I cut through the food court on my way out and spied Dylan with Meredith and the Sneakerocity boy, who actually *was* really cute. I paused and watched them for a minute, and I had to hand it to Dylan. The skateboarder guy was leaning toward her, listening intently to what she was saying and then laughing appreciatively at her comments. Meredith looked happy for Dylan, and Dylan looked ecstatic and kind of charming. I couldn't help but smile. I guess it does pay to have plans when you are interested in a boy. Social opportunities don't always happen spontaneously, though they just did for me.

Dylan looked up and caught my eye. I hesitated, assuming she'd look away, but I was so happy, I decided to wave and smile.

Dylan smiled too! And she waved back, a hearty wave even, and the cute guy turned, and after asking Dylan a question, he also waved. Meredith made funny gestures behind Dylan's and the guy's backs, like, *Get a load of these two*, and I laughed and waved again, then left, feeling happy for everyone.

Remembering my manners, I stopped at Olde Towne Bakery on the way to the exit and got some pastries and brownies to bring to Mia's dad as a host gift. I was happy I had the Soapy Chic creams for me and the other girls. I tucked my shopping bag into the bakery bag.

My dad was waiting by the curb when I got outside. We hustled home, and I raced around grabbing the things on Mia's list. I hesitated as I tried to decide whether or not to change my un-me and uncomfortable outfit. After all, Mia had said it looked good, and we *were* going to the city. But Dylan might kill me for taking her clothes, even though she'd insisted I wear them. Hmm. I decided to split the difference and kept the cropped pants but ditched the itchy sweater, replacing it with a long button-down shirt I'd been saving for a special occasion. With little flats and a cardigan, I had to admit, the new outfit looked pretty cute too.

My dad gave me some spending money at the train station, and, of course, I had my own savings, though I didn't know how much I'd be spending. I had never spent any time with Mia's dad, so I didn't know whether or not he'd be the kind of parent who never lets you pay for anything. (Lucky for me, it turned out he was!)

Mrs. Valdes pulled up behind us in her chic Mini Cooper, and Katie and Mia hopped out, dressed in even cuter outfits than before (thank goodness I'd tried a little harder than usual), and while we girls chatted, our parents discussed details and exchanged phone numbers and all that stuff.

I couldn't believe how much Katie and Mia had planned for the trip! They had every minute mapped out. I just hoped I could keep up.

"How do *you* know the city so well?" I asked Katie.

"Oh, I've been there a bunch with my mom over the years. . . ."

"But she's never been with *me* before! I've been telling her about all these places for ages, and I can't wait for her to finally see them. Oh . . . and you, too, of course!" said Mia.

I smiled and pretended I hadn't noticed the slight. *It's okay,* I told myself. *These two have had this plan for weeks, and you've been a part of it for only an hour and a half. Relax.* But I did feel a tiny bit uneasy about my role here. Like the afterthought that I was.

The train pulled into the station, and we squealed again.

"Okay, *mis amores!*" said Mrs. Valdes. "Have a beautiful trip! I know how happy Mia is to have you girls come see her other life!" She gave us all big hugs and kisses, and then my dad grabbed me for a tight squeeze and a kiss on the head.

"Have fun, kiddo," he said with a wink. "Text me when you get there."

And we waved and hopped onboard just as the doors began to ding their warning.

The train was pretty empty, so we quickly found three seats together for the ride. Two seats were side by side, facing two others, and without thinking, I let Mia and Katie sit next to each other and took the seat opposite, illuminating the fact that three is a tricky number.

"Okay, let's review the agenda, girls!" said Mia, pulling out a notebook filled with scribbles and clippings. She flipped to a page and began to read from it.

I pulled out my planner and flipped right to my list of things to do in New York City! "Oh, this is great, because I totally have this list of things to do in NYC, right here in my planner! So . . ."

"Yeah, well . . ." Katie and Mia exchanged an uncomfortable look. Mia spoke again. "See, we've kind of had this trip planned for a while, so . . ."

"What Mia's trying to say is we already have an agenda!" said Katie brightly. "So if your stuff fits in, then we can totally do it. Like, if it's on the way to where we're going, then by all means . . ."

"Yeah!" agreed Mia.

"Oh, right. Of course. Ha-ha. Duh!" Luckily, the planner is also my scheduling bible, so I just flipped to the page for today (which was mortifyingly empty), slid the pen out of its slot, and sat poised to take notes on what Katie and Mia had planned for themselves and now me. I chewed on my pen cap while I awaited further information.

"Okay!" continued Mia, looking at *her* agenda. "So today . . . we get there, leave our stuff at my dad's, and head out for a quick whirl around the neighborhood stores while we wait for Ava to get out of school. . . ."

"Oh, we're seeing Ava?" I asked, feeling relief. We'd all met Mia's best friend from when she lived in the city. She was nice, though I'd never had a chance to get to know her well. However, I was happy she would change our number from an awkward three to a more comfortable four. I just wondered who would pair off with who, because that's how foursomes work.

"Yes, she'll sleep over with us at least tonight, too," said Mia.

I looked at Katie, who was smiling a little too brightly. I was confused. "Are you really good friends with Ava too?" I asked.

Katie was taken aback. "Me? What? Oh, no. I've only just met her when you have. I don't really know her that well," she said.

"I mostly spend time with Ava one-on-one," said Mia with a shrug. "I've just always kind of kept things separate, I guess."

"Oh, so like when she comes out to visit . . . ?"

"Mostly I go in to visit her," said Mia. "But

when she comes out, we just lay low, you know?"

I glanced at Katie, who looked a little hurt. "Oh," I said, suddenly understanding that it would be hard to be best friends with someone who already had a best friend from somewhere else. Poor Katie. "Right," I said. Emma might be away for the weekend, but at least she wasn't off with some other, potentially cooler, best friend she'd known for way longer. That would be hard. I chewed my pen cap again. "Okay, back to the plans . . . ," I prompted.

Katie laughed. "Oh, Alexis, you do love plans!"

"I like business plans when I make them and social plans when other people make them," I said. *And I've been sitting home alone for the past thirty-six hours,* I wanted to add, but I knew that would be a touchy subject.

Mia continued, "Okay, so we'll go surprise Ava around the corner from her school, which is my old school. Then we're going to go get this killer hot chocolate at City Bakery. It's so thick, it's like melted candy bars, and they have huge homemade marshmallows they put on top, and churros if we want them, for dipping."

"Yum!" I said, scribbling "Pick up Ava. Get HC. Churros!" in my book. "Do they have cupcakes?"

"Of course!" said Mia.

"You're always thinking about the competition!" teased Katie.

"Business first, that's my motto!" I said, and we giggled.

"Next, we'll walk home and pass by the baking store Katie wants to check out"—they exchanged a smile—"then we'll look into just one or two boutiques I like along the way, then go home to change and wait for my dad."

I scribbled furiously. "Will Ava already have her bag with her?" I asked.

"What? Oh. Well, maybe not, because it's a surprise that we're going to school," Mia said, a little distressed.

"Okay, just planning ahead," I said. "Emma always hates it when I forget to tell her to pack a bag in case she sleeps over. Then we're always scrambling at the last minute . . . you know."

"Right. Then we're going to dinner at Omen, that awesome sushi place in SoHo I've told you all about!" Mia's eyes lit up in excitement.

"I can't wait!" said Katie, grinning.

"Oh, is it cool?" I asked.

"Wait, you haven't heard Mia going on and on about Omen?" Katie laughed incredulously.

I shrugged. "I guess not," I admitted.

Mia giggled. "Well, after tonight we'll *all* be going on about it!"

I am personally not a fan of raw fish, but I felt like it really wasn't my place to throw a wrench into the plans. I made a mental note to eat an extra churro at the bakery.

"After Omen, my dad is going to take us to get our palms read by this really cool lady he knows."

"Wait, whoa! Palm reading?" That kind of stuff made me a little nervous. But Katie and Mia looked at me blankly, like, *What's not to like about palm reading?* "I mean, uh . . . wow!" I corrected, and they smiled.

"Yeah, she only gives out good news, though, so don't worry!" reassured Katie. "At least that's what Mia always says."

Mia nodded. "Right. Then after that we'll walk a couple of blocks to the treat that Katie and I have lined up to surprise you and Ava. . . ."

"What is it?" I asked excitedly.

They laughed. "We can't tell you! It's a surprise!"

"Oh." I felt a little left out. I guess I'd feel better after we hooked up with Ava. Then she and I could be left out together. I decided to change the subject. "Okay, and will we set up the beds before or after we go out?" I asked.

Mia laughed again. "You and your details, Alexis! I don't know! Before? After? Who cares?"

"Oh, I just thought 'cause maybe we'll be so tired when we get back . . ."

"No way. We will be rowdy!" said Katie, giggling.

"Okay . . . ," I said, and wrote in my planner: "Omen, palm reader, shop, get rowdy."

Katie leaned across the seats to see my planner. "Did you actually just write 'get rowdy' in there?"

I nodded. "Yes. Failing to plan is planning to fail!"

"How can you fail at being rowdy?" asked Katie.

"You can use up all your energy too early and then want to go to sleep when it's rowdy time, that's how," I said huffily. Didn't everyone know that?

"Alexis Becker, you are too much!" said Katie with a laugh as we entered a dark tunnel.

"The Beckers try harder." Mia giggled as she quoted our family motto.

It hurt my feelings a little, but I took a deep breath and decided not to turn their teasing into a fight. After all, it would be two against one. Not my favorite odds.

"And what's wrong with that, my friends?" I asked. "What's wrong with that?"

CHAPTER 4

New York's Best Hot Chocolate

$\mathcal{I}$ was overwhelmed just finding our way out of the train station, and I couldn't believe how confidently Mia managed the whole thing. We were weaving in and out of people in Penn Station and then onto a subway, then off a subway, then upstairs, downstairs, upstairs. And she knew where she was going the whole time! I may be a leader when it comes to business, but Mia is a leader when it comes to travel, that's for sure! Even crossing the street, Katie and I were chatting at one point and weren't paying attention. Mia had to stick her arm out to keep us from being run over by a turning taxi.

"Phew!" I said. "Thanks!"

"You've got to pay attention," cautioned Mia. "I

have to get you girls home in one piece!"

I was impressed. Just a few hours ago my mother was reprimanding me for walking alone in the mall, and here was Mia, navigating the subway and the city. I suddenly remembered I needed to text my dad.

We r in the city. Having a gr8 time!

We made our way to Mia's dad's apartment, which was downtown, according to Mia. It was kind of weird to think of living in the city, but I guess to Mia it was just normal. I, for one, could never get used to the noise of the traffic and the bustle of the sidewalks and the constant activity. It was so foreign to me. It seemed Katie felt the same way. She and I couldn't stop staring at people—a guy with a Mohawk and tattoos, a homeless lady in layers of rags, a mom pushing triplets in a stroller. There was so much to see!

Mia laughed at us as our eyes bulged out of our heads. "Guys, don't stare!" she admonished us in a whisper. "It's rude. And sometimes people get mad, like, 'Yo! What are you lookin' at?'" she joked in a thick New York accent.

Katie's eyes were wide. "But how can you *not*

look? I just cannot stop staring at everyone!"

Mia shrugged. "It's just, like, *whatever*, to me. To each his own."

"Huh," I said, still boggled.

We dropped off our stuff at Mia's dad's place, which was very cool. He's an architect, and his apartment looked like something you'd see in a magazine—all sleek. Then we headed out to meet Ava. Mia walks pretty fast, so I was hustling to keep up with her, and Katie was lagging way behind.

"Come on, chicas!" Mia called over her shoulder. "City pace!"

Katie and I looked at each other, and it was obvious we both wanted to roll our eyes, but neither of us wanted to gang up on our hostess. I knew then, though, that Katie and I would have to stick together. After all, it would be two city girls and two suburban girls. We'd be the new clueless ones, the ones doing everything wrong, like staring, walking too slowly, not paying attention.

We rounded a corner and saw throngs of kids pouring out of a building up ahead.

"This is it!" chirped Mia. "My old stomping grounds! Let's wait here." She stopped at the corner.

Katie and I started to chat idly about school, but Mia kept interrupting to point out people.

"Hey, see that lady crossing the street over there? That's my old math teacher. Supermean!" or "Oh! Look! There's my best friend from kindergarten, Jack Sproule! I haven't seen him in ages."

"Do you want to go closer, so you can talk to people?" I suggested, but Mia declined.

"No way. It was great leaving most of these people. And there's no point going back, because people will make a big deal that I'm there, and then we'll be stuck with a huge group."

Katie and I glanced at each other. "O-kaay. If you're sure . . . ," we said.

Mia continued to watch the crowd, like a hawk. It did seem as if she was kind of wistful, like she wanted to still be a part of it all. Shortly, Ava emerged with a pack of kids. Mia started yelling her name and waving wildly.

"Avy!" Mia yelled.

"Mimi!" Ava cried as she spotted us. The two of them began running toward each other.

They united in a big hug, wagging side to side really hard. I was smiling so hard, my face hurt, and I wondered again how Katie must feel right now, but I didn't want to turn to stare at her. Eventually, Ava and Mia separated, but they were still holding hands when they came over to us.

Ava gave Katie a hug and a grin and then gave me a kind of half hug, too. It was awkward, because I am not a big hugger, and I don't really know her, anyway, but we laughed. It was nice to see her.

"Are you ready?" asked Mia.

"Ready for anything!" Ava declared.

"Did you bring your bag?" Mia asked, looking around Ava to see if she had it in her other hand.

"My bag?" asked Ava blankly.

"For sleeping over!" said Mia, exasperated.

"Oh! Was I supposed to bring my bag?"

"Duh!" teased Mia.

"Sorry!" said Ava. "Well . . . maybe I can go home and just catch up with you guys later?" She seemed kind of bummed, and to me it seemed pointless.

"You can borrow some of my stuff," I offered with a shrug.

"Yeah, me too," said Katie. "Don't go home."

Ava laughed. "Okay! But I do wish you'd told me you were going to meet me at school—I have a sweet outfit all planned out for dinner. Anyway, where are we off to now? The usual?"

"You know it!" said Mia as we started to stroll away from her old school.

Katie and I looked at each other.

"Um, is the usual that churro place?" I asked.

Ava laughed again. "Yes. At only the best bakery in the city!"

"Well, it depends on what you're having . . . ," said Mia seriously.

"Okay, the best hot chocolate place in the city, then," said Ava confidently.

"For cupcakes, you have to go somewhere else," said Mia, turning to us.

"Like where?" I asked.

Here, Katie actually took the lead and began ticking off places on her fingers. "Magnolia Bakery, of course, then its offshoots: Buttercup Bake Shop and Billy's. Then there's Sugar Sweet Sunshine. Oh, and Baked by Melissa for minis. William Greenberg's. Eleni's. Yura. Crumbs for major toppings . . ."

"Wow!" I said. "I'm impressed. You don't even live here!"

Katie laughed. "My mom and I have done the cupcake tour of New York City a couple of times. I do consider myself a local expert." She pretended to fluff her hair in a joking, show-offy way, and we all laughed.

"I defer to Katie when it comes to New York City baking! No one knows more!" said Mia.

I happened to glance at Ava and saw her wince

a little. Yikes. All these different friendships were kind of a minefield. As soon as you were making one friend feel good, it turned out you were hurting another.

"Ava, what are you the expert on?" I asked lightly.

"Me!" Mia declared, and we all laughed again, but for Katie it was definitely a little forced.

"Well, I am an expert on Korean food, since it's my heritage, and I'm an expert on bookstores. And coffee shops—"

"And hot chocolate!" interrupted Mia, turning to open a door and lead us inside City Bakery.

The cavernous space was dark and industrial-looking, and pretty crowded for a random weekday afternoon. The cases held rich, gooey treats, and most tables along the sides were filled with young, cool-looking people.

"I'll grab a table! Order me the usual and I'll pay you right back!" Mia directed Ava.

"Got it!" agreed Ava, like this was a familiar drill. Ava led me and Katie to the back to order, and she filled us in on the choices.

"We used to always come here after school on Mondays to start off the week on the right foot. Mia used to get just regular hot chocolate—oh, you'll need to add some sugar to it, because it's pretty strong—and then one day the cute guy who knew us by that point basically forced her to try the Mexican hot chocolate. It's a little spicy, a little cinnamony, and it has a kick. Well, that girl has never looked back. No more Swiss Miss for her! Hey, Hector!"

The order taker knew Ava, and she said, "Guess what? Mia's here!" Hector gave her a free cookie to bring to Mia and made Ava promise to have Mia come back to say hi. Ava introduced me and Katie, saying, "These are my friends from out of town. Make sure their hot chocolates are off the chart!" Hector promised he would. I felt all cozy with Ava introducing me as her friend. It felt good to have this little circle of Mia being my friend, Ava being her friend, and now Ava being my friend. I couldn't tell if Katie liked it or not, though, because she was busy scrutinizing all the baked goods.

"I just can't believe the variety!" said Katie, astounded.

I was shocked by the prices. "Their profit margin must be huge!" I marveled as we snaked through the line and waited for our order to be ready.

"I know, right?" Ava said. "It's crazy. Places like this are a treat, though. You couldn't come every day. There are lots of treat places in the city and lots of cheap places. You just have to know when to splurge. Also, people tend to make more money in New York City than in other places, so they spend more. It does kind of balance out."

"Good point," I said. "I love economics."

"Oh! Me too!" agreed Ava with an excited smile, and we started talking about stuff we knew about business and pricing and trade.

Katie listened in silence as we chatted. I saw her look away toward Mia, who was on the phone—probably with her mom or dad—and then back at us. I tried to include her by explaining what we were talking about, but she didn't really get it.

"Anyway . . . ," I said, trying to wrap it up so we could include Katie in our conversation, but Ava kept right on chatting; she obviously didn't meet many other kids who were interested in economics. Luckily, Hector returned with our hot chocolates and churros, and we went to pay. I was truly shocked by the total, but Ava promised me I'd get what I had paid for, and she was right. The cocoa, served in little white bowls, was thick and rich (could they have used hot cream instead of milk?), and the chocolate was intense. I did end up adding a little extra sugar, but the big rectangular marshmallow they gave me made a delicious sugary life raft floating on top. The crunchy, cinnamony churro was delicious dipped in the hot liquid. I had such a major sugar-and-caffeine rush when I was finished that I didn't think I'd even be *hungry* by dinnertime, never mind worrying about sushi!

Mia and Ava caught up while Katie and I people watched and ate mostly in silence.

"We could own a place like this one day!" I said to Katie.

"Yeah." She nodded. "But not here."

"No," I agreed.

"I don't really like the city that much," she whispered. "It's kind of . . . intimidating."

"Yeah, it's a lot to handle," I admitted. "I can't believe Mia lived here."

Katie nodded again.

"What are you two whispering about?" interrupted Mia.

"Oh, we're not really whispering," I said. "We're just saying we can't even imagine what it would be like to live in New York City. It's overwhelming!"

Mia and Ava exchanged a proud look. "Well, people are born New Yorkers. Not necessarily in New York, but the ones born elsewhere find their way here. That's what my mom says."

"I can't imagine living anywhere else," said Ava. "I would not want to."

Mia bristled a little. "Not everyone has a choice," she said bitterly.

Ava looked instantly contrite. "I'm sorry, Mia! I know. I know." She patted Mia's hand. "Now go say hi to Hector, so we can get out of here."

Mia agreed and went to thank Hector for her freebie.

Ava turned to us quickly and asked, "How is she doing? Really?"

Katie and I were confused for a minute. "She's fine," I said. "Why?"

"No, I mean"—Ava bit her lip—"she's kind of a fish out of water there, right?"

"Not really," said Katie.

"It's not *Little House on the Prairie!*" I cried.

Ava laughed. "No, but Maple Grove *is* different. A lot . . . slower. You have less independence. You know." She shrugged. I thought about us walking around the city. Even Mia's mom didn't let her go to the mall alone.

"She's fine. She's doing great, actually," said Katie proudly. "We have our cupcake business. Then she tried out for the chorus, and she joined the newspaper. . . ."

"Really?" Ava looked surprised. "Wait. Wow. I didn't know all this, besides the cupcakes, obviously."

"I'm sure she meant to tell you . . . ," I said, not wanting Ava to feel left out. "You know how it is . . . when someone's out of your day-to-day life, you just forget—"

"We are still in each other's lives every day," said Ava firmly. "We text *every. Day.* "

"Oh. Sorry. Okay. Well . . ." I didn't know what to say, and luckily, Mia returned.

"You didn't tell me you'd joined the newspaper!" said Ava a little accusingly as we all stood and gathered our things to leave.

"I didn't? Oh! Silly me! I thought I had!" said Mia.

"So tell me now!" They linked arms, and Mia chatted and chatted as Katie and I followed behind, careful not to stare, careful to look both ways, and careful to walk as quickly as the two native New Yorkers. Katie and I didn't always agree on everything, but in this case we did—we both wanted to fit in!

CHAPTER 5

A Good Omen

We decided to skip our earlier plans and head directly back to Mia's apartment since Ava needed to borrow some clothes for our dinner out. Back at the apartment, we all piled into Mia's Paris-themed bedroom, which is pink and black and very cute. She has two beds, and her dad had left two air mattresses in bags for us to blow up, and two sets of cute sheets. We'd have to do that right before we left for dinner, though, or the mattresses would take up the whole room. Her room in Maple Grove is about four times bigger than the one in the city.

"I call sleeping in a bed!" cried Ava upon seeing the air mattresses. She flopped across Mia's extra bed and wiggled her legs in the air.

Katie and I looked at each other and shrugged.

"I don't mind an air mattress," I said.

"I don't think I do either. Should I?" asked Katie, smiling.

"I don't know. *Maybe it's a little countryish to sleep on an air mattress,*" I whispered as Ava and Mia began to unpack Mia's clothes.

Katie giggled and so did I. I didn't want to gang up or continue to draw lines within the group, but Katie and I did need to stick together.

"What are you two giggling about over there?" asked Mia.

"Nothing!" we said in unison, and laughed again.

I went to put the pastries for Mr. Cruz in the shiny black-and-silver kitchen and realized I still had the Soapy Chic hand creams in there. I took them out and held them in my hand. Should I just give them out now and give Emma's to Ava? Or would that be disloyal? Hefting them, I thought for a minute. Hmm. Emma would love it. I decided to wait. *I'll just save them for another time,* I figured, and returned to Mia's room to put them back in my bag. The other three girls were looking for an outfit for Ava to wear out to dinner.

"Hey, I have some stuff too, Ava. You're welcome to it," I offered. I knew I'd feel discombobulated if I arrived at a sleepover without any clothes. I unzipped my bag and began laying out the clothes I'd brought.

Ava came and looked them over. "Oh, that's okay, Alexis. I think I'll just borrow some stuff of Mia's," she said. "Thank you, though."

"What about this?" I asked, and I lifted up a navy turtleneck with thin, white, horizontal stripes on it. "This would look so cute on you!"

Ava scrutinized it and then shook her head. "Thanks. I'm okay. Really."

I put it back into my bag and shrugged. "Okay," I said.

Ava opened Mia's closet and started flipping through the hangers. "Where's that really cute gray dress of yours? The one with the purple trim?"

"It's at home," Mia apologized. "Sorry."

"Hmm. What about the neon-yellow jeans?" asked Ava.

"Also at home." Mia shrugged.

"By the way, 'home'?" said Ava indignantly. "I thought *this* was home!"

Mia laughed uneasily. "Yeah. My other home. I have two homes."

Katie and I exchanged a glance. It would be hard to be in Mia's situation.

"What should I wear?" Ava asked Mia.

Mia tipped her head to the side. "Well . . . I thought Alexis's turtleneck was cute. Kind of Parisian; you know, the stripes. With"—she jumped off her bed and pulled a pair of jeans from a shelf in the closet—"here. These are too small for me. You could fit into them for sure, and maybe do a big cuff at the bottom to turn them into capris. Then we'll add a jacket and maybe even a beret. Very chic. Very SoHo."

Ava squinted at my turtleneck again. I wasn't about to lift it up and offer it to her after she'd just rejected it. She could go get it herself.

"Well . . ."

I stayed totally neutral, sitting on the floor by my bag. I didn't care for my taste in clothes being evaluated a second time.

"Fine," said Ava.

"Fine"?

Katie was laying out her outfit now—a cute flouncy skirt, a shiny top, and ballerina flats.

"Pretty!" I said, and Katie smiled.

Ava and Mia came over. "I'd maybe tone it down a little," Ava suggested. "This place is stylish, but it's laid-back. Like, exposed brick walls and stuff. Plus, downtown is always way less dressy than uptown."

Katie's face reddened a little. "Oh," she said. "I thought it was supposed to be nice."

Mia looked like she felt bad and stepped in to soothe Katie's feelings. "No, it is nice. It's . . . The food is incredible, it's impossible to get a table, the people who work there are really helpful, and all the food critics eat there. It's a really nice restaurant. It's just . . . not dressy, you know? It's all about the food, and it's sort of a casual look, otherwise."

"Okay," said Katie. "So what should I wear?"

Mia looked into Katie's bag. "Well, this would be good!" She pulled out jeans and held them up against the shiny blouse. "Or this . . ." She held up a white T-shirt against the skirt. "Just go high-low, you know? Top fancy, bottom casual, or vice versa. It's all about the mix."

Katie breathed a sigh of relief. "Okay. So you think I'm okay?"

"More than okay," reassured Mia.

"And wait till you try the food!" said Ava. "They have the best sashimi . . . and there's shabu-shabu."

"No way! Shabu-shabu! You didn't tell me that, Mia!" Katie exclaimed.

Mia laughed. "That's 'cause I never get it. I'm always too stuffed with sashimi."

Huh?

I had no idea what these people were talking about. They could have been speaking Japanese for all I understood. (Actually, they basically *were* speaking Japanese.) But Katie is a major foodie who wants to be a chef and has already gone to cooking camp. She knows all about Japanese food and will try anything, anyway. I'm a little more conservative in my tastes, and I was too embarrassed to ask what on Earth they were talking about.

"Well, we'll all need to save room for the surprise Mia and I have planned for after," said Katie.

Just like I did, Ava asked, "What is it?" Katie laughed. "We can't tell you, silly, 'cause then it won't be a surprise."

"Oh. Am I the only one who doesn't know, though?" asked Ava.

I waved from across the room. "Nope. I don't know either."

"Oh. Okay," said Ava.

"We're clueless together!" I added, and Ava smiled.

Mia went to take a shower, and Ava and Katie started a little side conversation about cooking, and I just sat there and listened. Luckily, Mia called out for who was next to take a shower, and I jumped up and ran in.

Later, after we were all changed and taking turns primping at Mia's white vanity table, her dad came home, and we all went out to say hi.

Mr. Cruz is very handsome, with black hair and flashing dark eyes; thick, black eyebrows; and these stylish black-rimmed glasses that would look majorly nerdy on my dad but are supercool on him. "Girls! *Hola!* How is everyone?"

Mia reintroduced me and Katie, since he doesn't see us much, and he made a big show over Ava, calling her "my old pal" and making her feel special. It probably felt a little awkward for Katie, but I thought it was nice of him to make sure Ava didn't feel left out.

We followed him into the kitchen, where he spied my pastry box and asked, "What's all this?" I explained, and he was really happy, saying, "Pastries are my kryptonite!" and patting his tummy. "Thanks, Alexis, that was very thoughtful of you."

I felt special and generous, so I added, "Well, they're from all of us."

"Thanks, girls. Now who's ready for Omen?"

"We are!" we squealed, but my dread increased as we went to find our shoes and jackets. I wished desperately that Katie hated sushi too, but I knew I was alone in this one.

❁

We took the subway to SoHo and bustled through the sidewalks to the restaurant, which was up a few stairs in an old building. Inside, it was as Ava had described it, with simple wooden tables and chairs and somewhat dim lighting and exposed brick walls. We were led right to our table in the back and settled in.

"We usually see a celebrity," whispered Mia.

I craned my head around to look, but Mia reprimanded me. "You have to act natural! They don't like it if you stare. I'll let you know if I see anyone."

I felt a flash of annoyance, as I am rather current on minor celebrities, due to my celebrity ballroom dance obsession, but I couldn't very well turn in my seat and watch the door for the evening.

"Now, should I order for the table . . . ?" asked Mr. Cruz, looking around.

I skimmed the menu and gulped. Steak was thirty-eight dollars. Organic chicken was twenty-eight dollars. This place was expensive! And I didn't dare make trouble by wanting something differ-ent from the others. Well, maybe they wouldn't notice if I didn't eat much. I was still okay from the churro, though surprisingly, the feeling of fullness was starting to wear off. Maybe it was the delicious smells coming from the kitchen.

The waiter came over to say hi and recognized Mr. Cruz. They began chatting, with Mr. Cruz asking what the waiter's recommendations were for the evening. They agreed on miso soup all around (I knew what that was! We have it at school sometimes!), then everything became unintelligible to me: mixed sashimi platter and shabu-shabu. Oh, whatever, I figured. I'd just deal with it when it arrived.

We chatted while we waited for our food, and Mia told her dad about our trip to City Bakery and our plans for the next day and night. Ava wouldn't be able to sleep over tomorrow because she had ballet, and frankly, I was relieved. I held myself back from yelling, "I call sleeping in a bed!" as Ava had done earlier, though I knew it would have cracked up me and Katie.

Mr. Cruz told us about his job and some cool accounts he was working on, and then he told us about all the art shows and performances he'd seen lately. He made it sound fun to be a grown-up living in New York. Maybe once you're older, it's not as intimidating. I don't know.

The soup was good, and the waiter also brought

some edamame, those little salty green soybeans you pop out of pods into your mouth. I am good with veggies, since that's practically all my (health nut) mom feeds us. But instead of making me feel full, the soup and the beans acted like teasers, leaving me almost hungrier than before I started. The others started to get excited for the sashimi, and I was in full dread-panic mode.

Finally, the waiter distributed small plates and white shiny chopsticks, and then another two waiters arrived with an enormous platter of what looked like little pastries or candies. But they weren't. It was all raw fish, cut up and folded into intricate designs and little sculptures, in different shades of white, pink, black, and gray. Some pieces had pale pink dust scattered over them, some had little tiny black or red eggs, and some even had tiny purple flowers on top. It was beautiful-looking, but my mouth just couldn't make the leap to wanting to eat it.

"Why don't I serve it out?" asked Mr. Cruz.

Katie, Mia, and Ava were practically levitating in their seats, squealing and pointing out things. I wasn't sure if I should copy them and act all excited or just play it cool. Which would make it less obvious that I had absolutely no plans to put any of this stuff in my mouth? I just plastered a fake smile on my face, like I was stunned by the artistic skills on display (I was), and left it at that.

When Mr. Cruz handed me my plate, there were five little items on it. I inspected them to see what they were, but I hadn't a clue. I do eat quite a bit of fish at home, but it's always cooked by the time I see it, so I couldn't even tell if these were things I'd normally eat cooked.

The other girls were oohing and aahing, so I kind of hammed it up a little too. I figured they all knew what everything was, so I was relieved when Katie asked Mr. Cruz to explain each of the items.

"It's almost too pretty to eat!" I said, and everyone laughed.

They dug in while I began to stress. I could feel my face turning pink, and I began lecturing myself in my mind. *It's just food. One bite won't kill you. Be a good sport. The Beckers try harder.* But in the end I copped out.

Spying an innocent young woman with blond hair entering the restaurant, I pointed her out shamelessly. "Hey, isn't that Taylor Swift over there?"

When everyone turned (nice job acting natural, people!), I slid a piece of fish off my plate and into my napkin.

Phew. One down and four to go.

I pretended to chew.

"No, I don't think so," said Mia, disappointed.

"Oh. Sorry. I guess I have celebrity fever," I said.

I toyed with another piece on my plate while the others wolfed theirs down.

"Do you like it?" Mr. Cruz asked me.

"If she doesn't, I'll have hers!" said Ava with a laugh.

"Oh, yes!" I lied, and nodded as I picked up piece number two and took a bite, because everyone was looking at me and I had to. The texture was odd, and the temperature was not what I'd expected, but rather than tasting fishy, the morsel tasted like the deep ocean—fresh, cool, salty, healthy. Huh. I couldn't say I liked it or wanted more, but for now, I had to say it wasn't awful.

A waiter, bless his heart, passed by with a steaming vessel of something, and everyone turned to watch him. Bingo! Piece number three went into my lap. I felt like a heel for wasting the fancy food, but I just couldn't face the shame of not being a sashimi eater in this group. Pretending to chew, I reached for my water and knocked the glass slightly, splashing water onto the side of my plate.

"Quick! Your napkin!" said Mia.

Right. Lifting the ball that was now my

fish-filled napkin, I knew it was decision time. Quickly, I opened it below the table and let the fish fall to the floor against the wall (sorry, Omen) and used the napkin to blot the plate. Phew. But the others declared my remaining two pieces of sashimi ruined.

"That's okay, I'm—" I couldn't decide if I should say I was full or saving room. It all depended on what the heck shabu-shabu was.

Luckily, the waiter arrived to clear our plates for the next course, and Mr. Cruz speared one of my sashimi as the plate was lifted. Only a few pieces of food wasted. I didn't feel too bad about that. It was a small price to pay for saving my reputation.

Well, it turned out shabu-shabu was beef strips you cook yourself by dipping them in scalding broth, and that was something I could really enjoy. By the end of the meal I was happy and chatting and feeling so relieved that I actually declared Omen my new favorite restaurant, causing Mia and Ava to squeal and hug me from either side. I felt like I'd passed a test, and it felt great.

"Well, I hope you saved room!" cautioned Katie as she and Mia exchanged a meaningful look.

"I am going to weigh three hundred pounds by the end of this weekend!" declared Mr. Cruz with a laugh as he signaled for the check.

As we thanked the restaurant staff and left, I glanced back to see the waiter stoop to pick up my fish from the floor. I gulped, sending him an ESP message of thanks.

Outside, Mr. Cruz asked in a spooky, joking voice, "And now . . . are we ready to learn our futures?"

We all cried, *"Yes!"* We set off for the palm reader's on the next block.

I just hoped that my future contained major success and very little raw fish.

CHAPTER 6

More Omens

Madame Khalil's Palm Reading Emporium was down a flight of stairs on another side street in SoHo. I would never have discovered her because there is no way I would have gone in there on my own. I am pretty brave when it comes to making contact with new people (I will always pick up a phone to make a call or whatever), but there is no way on Earth I would have gone down into this spooky little place.

As it turned out, neither had Mr. Cruz, originally. He'd been at a friend's party at a belly dance–themed restaurant nearby when Madame Khalil had arrived by prearrangement to read palms. She'd handed out business cards with hand maps on the reverse sides that showed how to find your lifeline and stuff, and Mia had been so enchanted when she'd seen it later at his apartment that Mr. Cruz had made an appointment and brought her.

I liked the idea of a palm reader with a good head for marketing and who also kept to a schedule. We were off to a good start, Madame Khalil and I, even though I am not at all one for these touchy-feely kinds of nonsense.

On our way, when Mia had asked who wanted to go first, I felt the need to redeem myself from the sashimi debacle, so I volunteered. The other two girls squealed and said they were scared, which made me feel good and brave. However, when we got inside, I started to have second thoughts myself.

The waiting area was dimmer than the brightly lit street, and heavily scented like smoked flowers. There were big, fluffy fake plants, and Indian art-work, and plump chairs covered in heavy tapestry fabric. There was quiet drumming playing over the sound system. I felt like I'd entered a foreign country until I noticed Madame Khalil had a computer and printer at her desk and also a credit card machine, so that made me relax a little. I could see for sure that I was dealing with a fellow business-woman.

After the bell on the door jingled our arrival,

there was a pause, and then a beaded curtain was pushed aside and out came a beautiful woman in a long, intricately decorated tunic, with jewelry on all of her fingers, wrists, ears, neck, toes—you name it. Her eyes were heavily made up, and she wore a small turban that covered the top of her head, while thick black hair hung down her back in loopy curls. She was beautiful but intimidating.

Mia smiled nervously, as she was the closest to the curtain.

"Hello and welcome, my friends," said Madame Khalil in a deep but melodious voice. "I am happy to see you." She nodded at Mr. Cruz, and he nodded back with a smile. "So it is just the four girls who will see me tonight, not the daddy, correct?" she asked.

"Correct," he said. "I know all I need to know for now."

"Wonderful. Then who would like to come see me first and learn the secrets the universe has in store for her?"

Ava and Katie pushed me toward Madame Khalil. "Alexis is first!" they cried.

My feet felt like they were made of lead.

"Do not be nervous, my young doe. My information will be beautiful, and you will enjoy it very much. Come. I can already see your aura, which is very strong. Very positive."

Gulping nervously, I took Madame Khalil's outstretched hand and followed her into her inner room. She shut the door after us, which made me panic a little, but she smiled and said, "Do not worry. It is all part of the show."

I laughed nervously. "The show?"

"Yes. People pay for the drama," she said wistfully. "They do not believe in my gift unless I make myself into a spectacle. It is very sad. But we are not here to be sad!" She snapped her fingers in the air. "Tonight we are here to unlock the joyful mysteries of your future!"

Yikes!

"Please to have a seat," she instructed me, gesturing to the chair across from where she lowered herself. She flounced her tunic and her hair out behind her as she sat, and a delicious scent of clove billowed out. It reminded me of baking, and I felt myself relax a little bit.

"Good. There, my pet. We are here for a nice time. If you relax, you will find it very pleasant, and perhaps you will not even want to leave!" Madame Khalil laughed prettily, and I sat back in my seat a little. "Now, let us start with your aura, which is very strong. Yes, *you* are very strong!"

I smiled a little, because I do like to think of myself as strong—somewhat on the outside, but definitely on the inside.

Madame Khalil continued, "Good! I see hard work. I see you are very organized. I see someone who is very thoughtful, thinking of others. But also I see . . . you are a little shy with your friends, no?"

Wow. That was fast. "Uh . . . yes. Sometimes," I agreed.

She spoke to me firmly, like she was lecturing me. "You are a leader. You must not feel shy. You have the very good ideas. People will like to follow you. But you must use your power for the good. Like me! Ha-ha-ha!" She chuckled again. "Now, please to give me your hand for a look."

I held out my palm toward her, and she lifted it gently. I wondered if this would take long or not. So far I liked what I was hearing, even though none of it was really a surprise to me. I just didn't want to hear anything too specific that would haunt me forever.

Madame Khalil made noises deep in her throat as she felt my palm and turned it from side to side to inspect it. "Hmm. Ah! Uh-huh. Uh-hmm. Ach. Ah. A la."

"Is it okay?" I asked nervously, unable to wait.

"Ah.Yes. It is very good.You are special. Do you see these lines? You will have many children. You will be a very good mother. Or maybe a very good teacher. It is unclear if they will all be your children or someone else's.You will be very successful. I tell you this already, no? Your aura, it is very strong. Now. Business. Hmm."

She started making the noises again, and I was all ears, not wanting to miss anything.

"You will start very young. You will be very successful. There will be a long break in the middle. Children, maybe. Or travel. Then more success.Your own business.Yes. Something with food, maybe, no?"

Wow! I couldn't help it. I laughed. "Maybe!" I said. Madame Khalil looked up and smiled.

"I am right, no? Madame Khalil is always right. Now. Your friends. You must be the peacemaker. You must not start trouble.You are on this Earth to end trouble. Do not seek it. Stay away from troublemakers.You must have peace for your success. *But* . . . I see a very, very busy social calendar. Lots of travel to New York City. Maybe even you will live here for a time.You are good with numbers, no?" she asked suddenly.

"Yes, I am," I admitted. "How can you tell?"

"Shape of fingers." She nodded, pleased with herself for being right.

"Does it say I will work with numbers?" I asked, disappointed in myself for so quickly believing all this hocus-pocus, but still wanting to know.

"Yes." Madame Khalil nodded again firmly, poking me in the palm. "Yes. Of this I am sure."

She seemed to be wrapping things up, and now I didn't want it to end. It was fun talking to someone who seemed to have all the answers and who seemed to want to discuss you and your future.

"Any advice?" I asked hesitantly. I didn't want to know anything specific, but what the heck!

Madame Khalil frowned. "Yes. Be sure to take your vitamins. Take care of your health, especially with sleeping."

Gosh, had my mother paid her to say that?

"Also, you will find yourself in the middle of things. You must be sure to keep things peaceful. And you must take more chances for yourself. Not for business. For you! For love! For fun! Try new things! Keep life interesting. Responsibility is yours for this. All work and no play is very bad for the heart line. Okay?"

I grinned. "Okay. Yes. Thank you."

"You are a good girl. I can see this. It is in your aura. Okay. Go and send in a friend. Good luck to you. Take a card. Visit my website, okay?"

I laughed and took the card. "Thank you."

Outside, the other girls jumped on me. "What did she say? What did she say? Was it scary?"

I blinked at the light, which was a tad brighter than in the inner room, though by no means glaring. I suddenly didn't really want to share the information. It was too new, and I hadn't processed it. I ached for my planner, which was back at Mia's. I wished I could log in all the comments, so I could and refer back to them later.

"Anybody have a paper and a pen? I need to write it all down in a list," I said.

The others groaned and pushed Ava in next.

"Pretty good, right?" asked Mr. Cruz with a laugh, offering me a pen from his pocket and a sheet of paper he pulled from Madame Khalil's printer tray.

"Yes, it was really good!"

"Then it's all true!" he said. "If it hadn't been good, I would have given you my whole it's-just-a-hokey-act speech."

"Oh, gosh no! Please don't do that!" I said,

laughing. "I want to believe it. Thank you!"

"My pleasure," said Mr. Cruz, his eyes twinkling. I wondered if he'd fed her any information about us when he'd made the appointment. Well, even if he had, it was okay. I liked what I'd heard.

We waited quietly in the outer room, and once we'd all cycled through Madame Khalil's inner sanctum, she came out to bid us good-bye. Or maybe for Mr. Cruz to pay. Either way, it was good to see her again, and I vowed in my heart that one day I'd return, with all my children and business success in the food industry, and after some travel.

As we exited, we all began to chatter at once, pleased with the plumping compliments Madame Khalil had privately bestowed upon each of us. Somehow she'd managed to get to the heart of each person's skills and attributes and make them feel very good about what they already had. Maybe there was more business sense in all this than I realized at the start. The best things in life take the basics and make them better.

Katie and Mia led the way to our next stop. I was starting to fade, as I am not used to walking this much or to staying up this late. I hoped "get rowdy" would fall off the to-do list by the time we got home. *I call sleeping anywhere,* I thought.

Ava and I trudged behind the "leaders" as we crossed a few blocks over to get to our next destination.

"I can't imagine where we are headed. I mean, there's nothing over here. This is like a wild goose chase," Ava muttered crankily.

"Well, I'm sure it's something good if we've come this far!" I declared. I didn't want to align myself with Ava just now since she was being so negative.

Finally, we turned down another cobblestone street, with more storefronts clad with flags and decked with black fire escapes. (The stores were all starting to look the same to me.)

"How can you ever find your way around this place?" I asked incredulously. "Everything looks the same!"

The others all laughed. "Alexis! That's not true!" said Katie. "Anyway, I love the walking. It makes me feel so alive!"

Katie, of all people! My fellow Maple Grover was now acting like a native New Yorker.

"Oh yeah, city slicker ..." I started to tease her a little, but then I remembered Madame Khalil's words about being a peacemaker. Quickly I changed my tune. "Then you're going to have to be my guide

73

and teach me all about this place because I am clueless!"

Mia laughed. "Alexis is never clueless! This is a treat!"

"Ha-ha," I said.

"Here we are!" cried Katie as she stopped in front of another tall storefront, this one with a line snaking out the door.

I craned my neck back to read the sign. "Georgetown Cupcake! No way! Like on the show!" I said.

Katie grinned. "You got it!"

"OMG. This is awesome!" I was really excited. I admire these sisters so much. They started this bakery that became this huge national chain. It's like they're living my dream, having it all and making so many people happy at the same time. *Hey, maybe that's why Madame Khalil thinks I'll be spending time around lots of kids when I grow up!* Cupcakes attract kids! And sure enough, even though it was pretty late, there were plenty of kids in line, yanking on their parents' hands and pointing at what they wanted. City kids definitely stayed out later than kids where I live.

Inside, everything looked so delicious, even the big mural of cupcakes on the wall, and the place was packed. I couldn't help counting the number of customers and multiplying by $2.75, the price of a cupcake (in the unlikely event people bought just one). With fifty people in the store at the moment, multiplied by basically three bucks, the store was making . . . only $137.50. Hmm. With four people behind the counter and rent and supplies . . . Not great numbers. *Maybe opening a cupcake store isn't the way to go,* I thought suddenly.

"Maybe we should get an assortment?" offered Mr. Cruz, interrupting my math reverie.

"Oh yes, Dad! But . . . let's let Katie order them, okay? Since she's the expert."

"Absolutely," agreed Mr. Cruz.

I glanced at Ava to see how she'd handle this, and her brow was a little wrinkled. "I've never been here. I think I read about it, maybe. I can't believe I've never been, though!" She seemed astounded by the fact Katie knew about it and she, the native New Yorker, did not.

"Don't worry, Ava, there are thousands of places I've never been in this city," said Mr. Cruz comfortingly. "It's so hard to stay on top of all the new stuff cropping up all the time."

"Yeah, but I can't believe *I've* never been!" said Ava.

"Hey, now you're here! Don't worry about it!" said Mia, joking, but it seemed to irritate Ava.

"Well, I would have thought you might have—"

I could sense trouble brewing, so I used my old trick again. "Hey, look! Taylor Swift!" And everyone turned again for a nanosecond and then started laughing.

"You're like the boy who cried wolf!" said Katie, shaking her finger at me.

"Yeah, I'm the girl who cried Taylor!" I said, and we all laughed. Phew. Crisis avoided. For now, anyway.

CHAPTER 7

Always Prepared

𝒯hank goodness we did not have to get rowdy when we got home. It was actually pretty late, and even Mr. Cruz was tired. He asked us all to get right to sleep, since we'd have another big day tomorrow, Saturday.

Finally, I was lying in the dark, snuggled under the covers and thinking over the day. It had been fun, but I wished Emma had been here to share it all with us. She never would have eaten sashimi, and the two of us would have been able to discuss Madame Khalil's predictions in-depth. "I wonder how Emma's doing," I said.

"Oh, yeah. Poor Emma with all those boys," Katie said with a moan.

"Well . . . except Matt," I cautioned, since I have

a huge crush on Emma's older brother.

"Right! Except Matt," amended Katie. "Sorry."

"And Sam!" called Mia from up in her bed. Sam is the oldest in Emma's family, and a supercutie.

We all laughed.

"And Sam," agreed Katie. "Oh, and that little Jakie is so adorable, we really can't forget him!"

"Oh, for goodness' sake, will you all please stop talking about people I don't know?" asked Ava, aggravated. She sat up and fluffed her pillow hard, almost punching it, then she lay back down with a huff.

There was a brief silence. "Sorry, Avy," said Mia. "Sometimes we forget."

"I don't think we talk about people you don't know *all* the time. Just occasionally, and then only by accident or necessity," said Katie quietly.

I agreed with Katie. Ava was being overly sensitive, but I didn't want this to turn into a fight. I had thought three would be a tricky number, but now I could see that numbers don't have much to do with anything. It all depended on who was in your threesome or foursome.

"It's just, none of us has any brothers, not counting Dan," I said. Dan was Mia's newish stepbrother. "So we're kind of fascinated by the Taylors." I thought maybe if I explained it a little, it wouldn't seem so exclusive.

"Yeah, well, I do have a brother, and I do not find him fascinating," said Ava crankily.

"What's your brother's name?" I asked Ava.

"Christopher," she said.

"Older or younger?" I asked.

"Younger," said Ava.

Wow, we weren't really getting anywhere with these one-word answers.

"Is he gross?" I asked.

"Yes!" said Mia. "Sorry."

"I guess so," said Ava. "Yes."

"What's he up to tonight?" I asked.

"Probably home watching sports with my dad," said Ava.

"Oh my gosh, he is sooo obsessed with sports." Mia laughed.

"Yeah," admitted Ava.

"I mean, he's good at sports too. It's not like all he does is watch them. Remember, we went to watch his basketball game that time . . . ," Mia reminisced.

Ava propped herself up on her elbow and finally laughed a little. "Yeah. And he made that three-pointer from across the court, and my mom screamed! That was so embarrassing!"

"It was hilarious! And he was, like, the champ of the game. His team picked him up and carried him around!"

"Oh boy, was he hard to live with after that!" said Ava.

I felt a little better now that I'd softened up Ava.

"That's like the time we went to Matt Taylor's game . . . ," began Katie.

Aaargh!

I wanted to crawl under my covers and stay there. She'd just undone all the work I'd done making Ava feel included. *You just can't win,* I told myself. Shortly after that we all fell asleep, thank goodness. At that point, there was nothing left to do.

The next day was beautiful, and we all woke up early, but Mia's dad had been up even earlier and had gone out to get us delicious bagels from around the corner. They were still warm and very soft. Katie and I couldn't stop oohing and aahing over them.

"These are good bagels," said Ava. "But the *best* ones are right by my apartment. Ess-a-Bagel, it's called. Those are *really* New York City bagels."

Katie and I glanced at each other, like, *What does it matter? These bagels are delicious.*

Mia changed the subject quickly. "So let's talk about what's on for today. Let me get my list."

She returned and began reading off agenda items. "Breakfast, check. Clean up and get dressed, almost check. Shopping around the Flatiron. Maybe cupcakes at Billy's in Chelsea. Stopping by that baking store you're interested in, Katie. Lunch at Shake Shack. Then MOMA. Look for Wayne Thiebaud pictures. Next, Magnolia, of course. Walk through the park. Then maybe Dylan's Candy Bar, for market research, of course. Plus, Katie there's that place you asked about. You know . . ."

Katie nodded. "Right! Got it."

I didn't understand half of what that girl had just said! MOMA? Thiebaud? Flatiron? "Whaaaaat?" I cried in frustration, and put my head in my hands. I looked up just in time to catch Ava rolling her eyes.

"Have you just never spent any time here before?" she asked icily.

"Well, we've come in to see a lot of Broadway shows," I said. I knew I was being defensive, but she was being . . . offensive, actually.

"But you live pretty close. You never come in for the day or anything? To shop?" Ava wondered.

I shrugged. "My sister comes in. I'm just not all that into shopping."

"Yeah," agreed Ava, looking me up and down as if to say, *I can tell.*

Well, look who woke up on the wrong side of the bed, I thought. *Should have tried the air mattress, missy.* But I thought of Madame Khalil again and bit my tongue.

"We should try to come in more," agreed Katie, stepping into the fray. "We just get so busy with work and school and little events and stuff out there that it never occurs to us to come in. It is fun, though."

"I still come in all the time," said Mia.

"Obviously," said Ava. "Now, do we have to go to all these bakeries today?"

Mia and Katie and I all looked at one another. I was feeling less enthusiastic about the cupcake retail business in general after I did my store math last night, but at the same time, I actually didn't want Ava to "win." (Isn't that terrible? And me, a peace-maker!) I also felt bad for Katie, who was honestly interested from a business standpoint but also as a true baker.

"Yes. We've had it planned for weeks," said Mia firmly. What she didn't say was, *You don't have to come,* but it was kind of clear that that's what she was thinking.

There was a silence for a split second, and then Ava said, "Okay. But then let's go to the new Sprinkles or to the Magnolia at Bloomingdale's. I haven't been up there in ages."

Mia looked at her and then said, "Let's play it by ear."

"I remember Emma mentioned the Magnolia at Bloomingdale's," I said. "She was in for a shoot or something for them, and she and her mom stopped in for a treat." (Emma models, and sometimes work brings her into the city.)

I thought I caught Katie and Mia exchanging a look, but by now I was so confused about all the alliances and enemies and different agendas that I just didn't care.

"I'm going to get dressed!" I announced, and I cleared my plate, went back to the room, and made my bed (aka air mattress), and got on my clothes. It felt good to be away from all the squabbling, even for a minute.

I took a deep breath and opened my planner, adding to the notes I'd made last night from what I could remember of Madame Khalil. Then I chewed on my pen cap. My parents always tell us, when something seems big and intimidating (like the rest of this trip), to break it down into smaller, more manageable chunks. So I just needed to get through this morning. Then lunch. Then the afternoon. After that, Ava would be gone, which would remove much of the tension but would return us to a threesome, which was still tricky, especially with Katie and Mia and all their inside plans and secret ideas. Then we had this evening and tonight and then home in the morning. It seemed like a lot, even in chunks. *The Beckers try harder,* I told myself. Sighing, I decided to turn it all into a game. Maybe for every fight I defused, I'd give myself . . . ten minutes of *Celebrity Ballroom* reruns when I got home! That ought to do it!

When I came back out, Mia and her dad were having a quiet chat in the kitchen, and I didn't want to interrupt. I thought I heard her mention Emma for some reason, and I kind of cringed. I didn't know how much Mia told her dad, but I just hoped she wasn't complaining about me missing Emma all the time. That would be embarrassing and make me seem ungrateful to Mr. Cruz for having me here, as if it wasn't good enough without Emma, too. I turned up the TV a little to drown them out and just sat and waited until everyone else was ready to go. I hoped it wouldn't be too long of a wait.

❀

Okay, I will say this: Shopping with Mia is kind of amazing. It's like magic. You walk into a store and quickly think, *Wow, there's nothing here for me. Nothing that would look good, nothing I could afford.* And then Mia walks over and picks up some random and cheap little scarf and drapes it on you in a certain way, with flair, and suddenly, you look like a star. Like Taylor Swift! Ha. That happened a lot, and though I didn't buy much, I could have.

We hit a bunch of places around the Flatiron (it's a district, or neighborhood, Ava informed me, that is named for a funny-looking building there shaped like an iron). There were the expected chain stores, like Anthropologie, but also lots of cool local boutiques and street vendors selling unique stuff they'd made. We made our way west, into the area known as Chelsea, and stopped for cupcakes (midmorning snack) at a place called Billy's Bakery. Mia's dad had one and then pretended to cast a spell on us, so we wouldn't want any more cupcakes.

"I'm with you, Mr. Cruz. All this cupcake mania is wearing me down," said Ava.

"It helps to have a theme," snapped Mia.

"Okay, you two!" I singsonged. *Ka-ching!* Ten minutes of *Celebrity Ballroom* for me!

We shopped on, hitting a cool kids' bookstore

called Books of Wonder and some baking supply stores for Katie (Ava waited outside), and we wound up in a long but fast-moving line for burgers at the Shake Shack, which is a hamburger stand in the middle of a park. Once we got our food and sat on a bench to eat it, I could not believe how delicious it was.

"Oh, boy. I wish Emma was here. She'd love this!" I said.

This time I definitely caught Mia and Katie exchanging a look.

"What?" I asked.

Katie took a deep breath. "It's just . . . Why do you always talk about Emma? Aren't we your best friends too?"

I was taken aback. "I don't mean it that way," I said. "I just . . . I know she'd love all this stuff, and I feel bad she's not here for it. Especially since we're all here making these memories, and we won't really be able to talk about it back home or she'll feel left out, you know?"

Mia looked down at her burger thoughtfully. "You know, it would have been more fun if it was the four of us," she admitted.

"It *is* the four of us!" snarled Ava.

Mia looked up, surprised. "Oh! Sorry. No, I

meant, the four of us from home. You're always here. It's just a given!"

Ava was huffy. "I might *not* always be here. You never know."

"Come on, Avy," said Mia, grabbing her in a sideways hug. "You're home to me, *mi amor!*"

"Hey, I thought *I* was home!" Mr. Cruz protested, and we all laughed. We'd kind of forgotten he was there, which is I think the best thing you can say about a parent sometimes.

"Oh, boy. So many people to please," said Mia, shaking her head. I felt sorry for her. It would be exhausting to have this ping-pong life, Mom to Dad, city to suburb, Katie to Ava. Phew.

"You don't have to please me, anyway!" I said cheerfully. "I'm about as pleased as I can be with this ShackBurger and my black-and-white shake!" (Ten more minutes of *Ballroom*!)

"Oh no, speaking of shakes!" cried Katie. Her shake had spilled. "Anyone have a napkin?"

"I do!" I yelled, and I hopped up to share the pile of napkins I'd grabbed.

"Always prepared," said Mia, shaking her head and laughing.

"You say it like it's a bad thing!" I said, kind of joking but a little hurt.

"It's a good thing," said Mr. Cruz. "Trust me."

"That's why we keep you around!" joked Katie. But it didn't really come out as a joke.

"Ha-ha," I said lamely, but there was an awkward silence, and I think everyone was wondering for a minute if that *was* why they kept me around. Or at least I know *I* was wondering.

"Why do you keep *me* around?" Ava asked lightly, but I could tell she was kind of fishing.

"Because you know me . . . You've known me longer than anyone, and you're fun," said Mia decisively.

"Ahem," said Mr. Cruz.

"Sorry, longer than anyone except my parents!" said Mia, laughing and shaking her head again. "You see? I can't win!"

"Okay, so why do you keep *me* around?" asked Katie.

"Because you're fun also, and you make me laugh," said Mia.

"And what about me?" said Mr. Cruz. "Why do you keep me around?"

"Because you pay for everything!" Mia giggled.

"Ohhhh!" said Mr. Cruz, pretending Mia had shot him in the heart, and then we all laughed. Another crisis averted.

CHAPTER 8

BFFs

We took the subway uptown and began walking up Sixth Avenue and suddenly, things began to look familiar.

"Hey! It's Radio City Music Hall!" I cried. "I've been there!" I was thrilled to finally have a point of reference, someplace to prove I'd spent *some* time in New York before. "We came in to see the Radio City Christmas Spectacular there once!" I looked proudly at Ava, as if to say, *So there,* but she was chatting with Katie and hadn't heard me.

"Isn't it a classic?" asked Mr. Cruz. "I just love it. I should take you this year, *mi amor,*" he said to Mia. "I'll get us some tickets."

Katie and Ava turned to see what he was so excited about.

"Oh, I'd love to see the Radio City Christmas Spectacular with you," said Mia.

"No way! This is a *Nutcracker* year!" exclaimed Ava, grabbing hold of Mia's hand and swinging it.

"Oh! *The Nutcracker!* I've seen that too, a few times. At Lincoln Center," I said. I practically felt like the mayor at this point!

"We always go," said Ava. "I haven't missed a year since I was three."

"Wow," I said.

"I'd love to go to both," said Mia diplomatically.

"What's *The Nutcracker* again?" asked Katie.

Ava's face lit up. "It is a great ballet about a Christmas party, where a girl gets a magical nut-cracker as a gift, and then she and her little boy-friend go on a ride to a magical land of sweets. The dancing is amazing, and the costumes are so, so beautiful, and the music!" Ava began singing and dancing along the sidewalk. She was actually pretty good. I noticed she didn't make fun of Katie for not knowing what *The Nutcracker* was. Still, I was trying to be the peacemaker. *Celebrity Ballroom,* I thought.

"Hey, that's right! You're a ballerina!" I said.

"Well, I study ballet," Ava admitted modestly.

"Oh, you should see her. She's amazing!" Mia said proudly.

"Gosh, I love dance. Of all kinds. Have you ever danced in *The Nutcracker*?" I asked.

"Well," said Ava, looking down shyly. "I might this year. I'll know soon!"

"Whaaat? Oh, Avy! You didn't tell me you'd tried out!" squealed Mia.

Ava blushed. "I didn't want to say anything until I heard."

"So when do you hear?" asked Mia.

"Next week!" cried Ava.

"Ooohh!" She and Mia held hands and jumped up and down.

"I tell you, walking down the street with this gaggle is pretty wild!" said Mr. Cruz.

"Oh, Papi, you ain't seen nothin' yet!" said Mia with a laugh.

I noticed Mia hadn't given Ava a hard time about not telling her what she was up to. I wondered if it was harder to be the one who leaves or the one who is left. I guess it's hard both ways.

At the MOMA, which turned out to stand for the Museum of Modern Art (I figured it out on my own!), Katie and Mia were obsessed with seeing paintings by this artist, Wayne Thiebaud, who was having a big show there. It turns out he's known for painting pictures of stuff in bakeries, like cases full of pies or slices of cake lined up on plates, and the paint's so thick, it looks like real frosting and real filling. The paintings were actually all delicious-looking, so it turned out to be a really fun show to see.

I wasn't that into the rest of the art, and luckily, neither was Katie. She and I kind of hung back while the New Yorkers, Mia and Ava, raced from room to room, visiting sculptures and paintings, like they were old friends. Mia's dad was into it too, which made sense, I guess, since he is an architect.

"I guess it would be pretty cool to grow up here," admitted Katie as we sat on a leather bench and watched Mia and Ava fearlessly go up to a tour leader and start asking questions.

"Yeah," I agreed. "It would be different, that's for sure."

We were quiet for a minute, and then Katie said, "What did Madame Khalil tell you about yourself that you didn't already know?"

I thought for a minute, then I looked at Katie and giggled. "Not much. What about you?"

She started laughing really hard. "Nothing! Isn't that funny?"

She started copying Madame Khalil, saying, "You have a very strong head line. You are very, very smart lady! I think you are getting the good grades in school, no?" The two of us were gasping from laughing.

Soon Mia and Ava spied us and came over to see what was so funny. But neither of us wanted to hurt Mia's feelings by criticizing Madame Khalil, so we said it was a little boy we spotted picking his nose who'd made us laugh.

Mia kind of laughed a little at that, and I, for one, felt bad about lying, but it had to be done.

"Mia, what was it like to grow up here? Compared to Maple Grove, I mean," I asked.

I don't think she was expecting the question, so it took her a little by surprise.

"Seriously? Or are you joking?" she asked.

"No, seriously."

She thought for a minute. "Well, here it's not as much about fitting in, so that's easier. You can do your own thing. But it's more about finding your way, which can be harder, because there are a lot more choices here than there, you know? Sometimes it's better to have fewer choices." She shrugged. "Sometimes not."

"Here is way more fun," added Ava. "No offense."

Katie and I looked at each other, then back at her. "None taken," I said.

"It's sort of like . . . New York has different things for different moods. If you feel one way, you do one thing; if you feel another, you do another," said Mia.

"Kind of like friends?" I asked. Everyone looked at me, so I elaborated. "Like, some friends are fun to do certain kinds of things with, and some friends are fun to do others."

"Yeah," agreed Mia. "Or maybe some friends get you to do one kind of thing, because you share those interests or maybe they push you to do things you wouldn't normally do, and other friends have other purposes."

We were all quiet, thinking about this. I don't think anyone wanted this time to ask what their purpose was in Mia's life. At least I didn't. What if she said I had no purpose? (Other than always being prepared, obviously.)

"Wow, I think this museum's making us think too much," said Mia. "Let's get out of here!" She jumped up and, with a grin, waved us on to find her dad.

I, for one, was sorry Emma had missed the Wayne Thiebaud show, but I wasn't about to say that out loud.

❁

We walked uptown a little more and cut through Central Park to get to Bloomingdale's. I'd never been before, but Emma had told me about it, and she was pretty impressed by its size and everything they had for sale. I'd also heard Dylan talk about it extensively, so I decided it would be a good place to buy her a souvenir.

Mr. Cruz told us he'd go have a coffee in the café and read the paper. He said he needed a break from all the girliness. We just laughed, and Mia told him he was lucky to get such an insider's view of the world of women. We would meet him in an hour.

I couldn't stop marveling at all the inventory they had in the store. I mean, they must have had millions of dollars of stuff just sitting there, waiting to be bought. I suddenly remembered that Ava was into economics, so we struck up a conversation about trade and importing and sweatshops, where they have kids sewing clothes for pennies a day in poor countries.

"How do you know so much about all this?" asked Ava. I could tell she was impressed, and it made me like her a little more than I had yesterday.

"Well, my parents are both in finance, so we talk

about this kind of stuff at dinner, at home."

"Me too!" exclaimed Ava. "My mom is in finance, so she reads us articles from the newspaper at the breakfast table, and then we discuss them."

Up ahead, I saw Katie and Mia swoop down on some cool clothes.

"Was Mia always really into fashion?" I asked. Part of me hated to admit Ava might be the expert on Mia; I didn't feel like giving her a bigger head than she already had on that subject, but part of me also felt like she did deserve some credit as Mia's oldest friend.

"Yes, always! Like, obsessed! My mom has pictures of us playing dress up in nursery school, and Mia is decked out. Full-on jewels, accessories, high heels, a purse, sunglasses—you name it!"

We started laughing, and Katie and Mia turned back. "What's so funny?" asked Mia.

"Oh, Ava's just telling stories about when you were little, how fashion obsessed you were."

"Ava?" a voice called from the other side of a display. "Avaluna Ahnamana-Maniac?!"

Mia, Katie, and I looked at one another in confusion, but Ava's face lit up.

"Caroleena-in-a-Betweena-Jelly-Beana Phelan? Where are you?" she cried.

What on Earth?

A tiny girl with flaming red hair and a zillion freckles popped out her head from behind a rack of clothes. "It's you!" she exclaimed, and then she raced out and flung herself into Ava's arms.

"Hiiiii-eeee!" squealed Ava, hugging this creature mercilessly.

"Where have you been all weekend? I've been calling and calling!" accused Caroleena.

"I've been . . . I've been around! Where have you been?" Ava asked.

Around? Mia, Katie, and I exchanged another look.

"I thought we were doing something after school yesterday, but then you took off! Since when do you just take off like that?"

"Sorry! I just . . . My friend surprised me. My friends, I mean," Ava corrected herself. "Here! Meet Katie and Alexis, and this is my old friend Mia I told you about, remember? Who moved away before you came?"

"Oh, right! I remember something about that. Hi!" said Caroleena.

"Something about that"? Poor Mia. I didn't dare look at her.

"Hi," we all said.

But Caroleena had already turned her back on us and was talking in great animation to Ava, as if we weren't even there.

"Well, you'll never believe this, but guess who I just saw downstairs?"

"No. Way," said Ava.

"Yes. Totally. And guess what she was wearing?"

"You're kidding!" said Ava.

"No, I am not. Guess where she was going?"

"No!"

I looked at Mia and Katie, to see if they were as confused as I was, and from the looks on their faces, I knew they were. But Mia looked more than confused. She looked annoyed.

"Ahem." She cleared her throat but not loudly enough. Ava didn't hear her.

"Ava," she said.

"Hang on one sec, this is major!" said Ava, holding up a finger but not even glancing at us.

Mia looked like she'd been slapped. She stood stunned for a second and then shook her head as if to clear it. "If you need us, we'll be in the denim section," she snarled, and, turning to us, she said, "Come on!"

Mia walked away from Ava in long strides. I scurried to keep up. Mia glared at me.

"Okay. Right." Katie and I followed Mia while she prowled aimlessly through Petites (we aren't) and Misses Sophisticates (we're not that either) and then finally into a cool department of jeans and T-shirts (aaaahhh). Pawing through the familiar items here seemed to calm her down finally, and then she wheeled around and said, "Is it just me or was that incredibly rude?"

"Um . . ." I wanted to be sympathetic, but I also didn't want to fan the flames. (Ten more minutes of *Celebrity Ballroom*, please!)

"Well?" Mia turned to Katie.

"Yeah, I guess so. Pretty much," admitted Katie. Now that she was the clear winner in the best-friend sweepstakes, she didn't exactly seem eager to collect her prize.

"Wow. I mean, I have never even *heard* of that girl. And she has clearly never even heard of me, which is just . . . shocking, really. And Ava had the nerve to just go on and on and that girl with her weird nicknames and whatever. *Aaargh!* It's just so annoying!"

"Well, maybe she's just—" I began lamely.

Mia wheeled on me. "I've had enough of your peacemaking! It can't be sunshine all the time! I'm sorry if you don't understand because you and Emma get along perfectly and never fight, but what's going on around here . . . well, it's just NOT. OKAY."

"Hey!" I said indignantly. "That's not fair! I never said Emma and I get along perfectly. And what do she and I have to do with this, anyway?"

"What do you have to do with it? Isn't it obvious? You're the lucky one in all this! You have your best friend. She's still in your class at school. She lives around the corner from you. You've been together for a million years, and you know each other inside and out. Your parents are best friends, and you'll probably marry her brother, and then the two of you will be related for real, and it's all so perfect, can't you see?

"But look at Katie! Dumped by her best friend, Callie, she takes me on even though I'm the new loser, and I've still got Ava, who's fighting her to be my official best friend all the time. And how about me? I don't know where to turn! I'm trying to make everyone happy all the time and show everyone a good time, and I am just so sick and tired of it!" And with that she burst into tears.

Katie and I stood there with our jaws hanging open. I'd never seen Mia lose her cool before, and I'd rarely, if ever, seen her cry. Katie and I looked at each other briefly, and then we went to Mia's side to hug her and pat her back.

"I'm sorry," Mia said through her tears. "It's just too much for me all the time. It's exhausting."

Suddenly, Ava appeared behind Mia. "Hey! I found you!" she said.

Katie and I looked at her, trying to send her a message to back off, but she didn't get it.

You could see the surprise on Ava's face when she realized Mia was upset.

"Who was that crazy girl?" demanded Mia.

"Um . . . what? We're . . . She's just a friend of mine. From school. She's new this year. . . ." stammered Ava, shocked by Mia's outburst.

"What, and suddenly you're best friends even though you've only just met?" accused Mia.

Ouch. I didn't dare glance at Katie to see how this comment went over. It had to have hurt a lot.

"So what if she is? Can't I make some new friends too, or do I just have to hang around and wait for you to come back? Anyway, you're importing friends now, so what do you really need me for, anyway?" asked Ava, and tears began to fill her eyes.

Oh boy. It was definitely time to be the peacemaker. "Okay, people," I said firmly. "Let's sum this all up, and then we can see what is going on. Mia, you're hurt because Ava has a great new friend—"

"That I've never even heard of!" Mia interrupted impatiently.

"Right. That you've never heard of. And, Ava, you're upset because Mia has new friends—"

"That I hear about all the time!" complained Ava.

"Right. And Katie's feelings are hurt, because she doesn't know where she stands with Mia. In Maple Grove she's Mia's best friend, but here . . . Ava is." I couldn't believe I'd said that out loud, but at least now it was out there. "And I talk about Emma too much. And"—I decided to go for it—"I don't really know where I stand with you two, Mia and Katie, because you're kind of a pair, and Emma and I are a pair. And also Mia and Ava are a pair. And this whole thing is just really awkward!"

We all stood there in silence for a minute, thinking. Then Mia said quietly, "It's just really hard."

"You know, I think we all just have too many friends," I said.

We laughed weakly.

I tried again. "Look, it's Taylor Swift!" And everyone laughed again, this time a little more. Better, but still not great.

I gave it one last try. "Um, not to make this all

about me, but do you really think I'm going to marry Matt Taylor?"

And then everyone was laughing hysterically, and things were definitely on their way to being better.

CHAPTER 9

I ♡ Dylan's Candy Bar!

Not to sound like Dr. Phil on TV, but of course the healing happened over cupcakes. For real! After the blowup, I quickly purchased a three-pack of adorable sorbet-colored tank tops that said I ♥ BLOOMIE'S on them for Dylan, and then we went down to the new Magnolia Bakery on the Third Avenue side of Bloomingdale's. (I mean, I wouldn't have known it was new, but Ava informed me it was, and I was happy to learn that tidbit from a native New Yorker. It was information I could casually throw around at home to make me sound knowledgeable.)

We each picked out a cupcake, our second of the day, and sat at a little counter by the window.

"This is delicious. Is anyone taking notes for the

PTA meeting menu?" I asked innocently.

"Oh, Alexis!" Katie groaned.

"Kidding!" I said. "Sort of!"

"Always thinking about business." Mia laughed.

"Someone has to!" I said. "By the way, I'm thinking cupcake wholesaling is the way to go. Much less overhead."

Ava nodded. "Yes, and less liability, less holding of inventory . . ."

"Oh no, here they go again," said Katie.

"Listen, I'd like to propose a toast," said Mia, holding her cupcake up in the air. "To three of my four best friends, we're sorry Emma isn't here, but thank you all for putting up with my craziness. Thank you for being great friends for different reasons. Thank you for understanding me."

We all clinked cupcakes. "Here, here," I said. "And to Mia, the hostess with the mostest!"

"Yeah, seriously, this has been great," agreed Katie. "Thank you so much."

"I can't believe how much we've done!" I said. "It doesn't seem like we've only been here for"—I looked at my watch—"twenty-six hours!"

"Is that all?" Katie laughed. "It's been so smooth, it feels like way less!"

Mia playfully swatted her with a napkin. "Not

funny," she said, but then she smiled.

Ava thoughtfully licked off a blob of frosting from her wrapper. "You know, Maple Grove is really nice and pretty," she said. "If I had to live in the suburbs, it would definitely be there."

"Thanks a lot," I said.

"No, for real. The people are nice, obviously, and it's not totally city obsessed, like a lot of suburbs are. It has its own stuff going on, too. And I hear it has great cupcakes." She grinned.

"Guys, I'm sorry for all the drama," Mia began.

But we waved her off. "We get it," said Katie. "It's fine."

"But I didn't mean to be so mean," said Mia.

"It's okay," I said.

Mia laughed. "No, that was the part where you were supposed to say, 'You weren't that mean.'"

"Oh. Okay," I said, still not saying it. I grinned evilly.

Now it was me who Mia swatted with her napkin.

"We still love you, Mimi," Ava said sweetly.

"Hey, why does Caroleena have such a long nickname and mine is so short?" said Mia, nudging Ava with her elbow.

"Oh, that? I'm just making up for lost time.

It doesn't mean anything. Anyway, yours is short because I need to say it all the time. Hers, not as much."

"Thanks . . . I think," said Mia.

"You're welcome."

"Aha! I knew I'd find you here!" We all jumped at the interruption, but it was Mr. Cruz coming to collect us.

"Are we ready to pack it in?" he asked hopefully.

But Mia had a glint in her eye. She looked out the big plate-glass window across Third Avenue.

"Just one more stop," she promised.

Okay, you can just forget about cupcakes. Yup. You heard me right. My dream of owning a cupcake business when I grow up is over for good. Because I, my friends, am going into *the candy business*!

Dylan's Candy Bar is the best store I've ever been in in my whole life, and that is no joke. It is a marketer's dream; a perfect union of product and design; and a genius, wild, brilliant, and crazy store filled with glorious items for sale, many of them proprietary (which means the store makes them, so they don't buy them from a middleman, and therefore, *ka-ching!* More money for the store!).

Here's how it goes: You walk in, and there is candy for sale everywhere. Every kind you have ever heard of and many, many kinds you have never heard of but will love, anyway. It is a place where people will buy and try anything, because what's the worst thing that could happen? It's candy!

The music they play is all about candy. The floors are made with floating candy in intricate patterns. There are candy mosaics on the walls and huge plastic lollipops and enormous decorative pepper-mints and giant chocolate things in foil wrappers that are as tall as I am, and a chocolate fondue foun-tain and an ice-cream bar and a bathtub—a whole bathtub!—filled with bubblegum balls! It's like a fantasy. Everywhere you look there are beautiful rainbows on clothing, bags, cosmetics—you name it. It's like a color explosion, a feast for the senses, filled with things you really don't need but must have immediately, because they are so yummy or cute.

I couldn't stop looking everywhere. Luckily for me I was not hungry for any more sweets, so I wasn't spending my money on one-pound bags of candy the way most of the customers were. I did buy a little coin purse for my sister, because, after all, it said DYLAN's on it, and then I bought one for myself, because it really was cute. But other than that I just admired the way the store had created a place where I wanted everything, though I needed nothing.

It was sort of like what I'd observed at Madame Khalil's. The best things in life take the basics and make them better. Basically, this was just a place to buy sugar, something you can already get pretty much anywhere, something everyone understands and wants. It wasn't that different from the Maple Grove Candy Counter. In theory, anyway. But this store took it to a level no one had ever dreamed of before. They made it beautiful and glorious. I wanted to do that too, someday. I knew there was money in it, of course, but the genius of it was that you didn't even think about money while you were here. That, my friends, is a great business!

While I was waiting for the others to make their purchases, I leaned against the stair railing and watched the shoppers. This one blond girl had a big basket filled with things—big stuff, fun stuff. Not just one-pound bags of candy, but a big pillow made to look like a pack of Reese's Peanut Butter Cups and fun pj's in candy patterns and giant lollipops in rainbow swirls. I was admiring her loot when she turned, and we looked right at each other. Oh!

OMG! My jaw dropped, and the girl smiled at me and gave a little wave as she knew I was realizing who she was.

It was Taylor Swift!

Right there shopping at Dylan's Candy Bar!

"Oh!" Quickly, I looked all around for my friends, but they were at the register downstairs on the basement level. *No!* This couldn't be happening! I was dying to ask for an autograph, but I had no pen! I wanted to run and get my friends, but I worried Taylor Swift would be gone by the time I got back. I was frozen in place, staring as she picked up a couple of final items and turned, smiling, to give her overstuffed basket to a salesperson who'd arrived to help her.

She reached into her purse to get out her credit card, and I searched wildly through the stairwell to the floor below for my friends, but I was out of luck. I couldn't see them.

"Please don't leave!" I begged quietly.

I dashed down the stairs two at a time, my shiny black Dylan's shopping bag swinging wildly.

Scanning the room, I quickly located Ava, Katie, and Mia on a long line to pay.

"Guys!" I shouted. Everyone in the store turned to look up at me, but I didn't care. I gestured wildly to the floor above me, mouthing the words *Taylor Swift!*

What? Mia mouthed back at me.

"Taylor Swift!" I stage-whispered.

Katie put her hand to her ear, miming that she couldn't hear me.

Exasperated, I took the last few stairs in a leap and ran across the floor to them.

Breathless, I called, "It's Taylor Swift!"

They all turned away, annoyed. "Ha-ha," said Katie.

"That's getting old, Alexis," said Mia.

"No! For real! I swear!"

"Come on!" said Ava. "At least think up a new one."

Now *I* was annoyed. "You know what? Fine. I'll hold your place in line, and you can go up and see who it is!"

Ava and the others rolled their eyes at one another.

"Go! For real! Hurry!" I said, jumping into place.

Finally, Ava sighed heavily. "Fine. But you guys owe me." She stomped off and climbed the stairs, not quickly enough as far as I was concerned. Her legs disappeared from sight for a second, then two, then five. *What is taking her so long?*

"Come on!" I muttered, willing her to reappear.

And suddenly she was back. "It's her!" Ava cried from the stairs. "It's really her!"

Katie and Mia looked at each other, dumbfounded.

I smirked. "See?"

Then they took off, and I wound up chasing them up the stairs.

"Hurry!" cried Ava. "She's leaving!"

By the time we got to the top of the stairs, all they got to see was a flash of blond hair exiting the store, and then a driver at the curb, opening the rear door of a white SUV with a flourish, and the girl—Taylor Swift!—climbing inside with two huge Dylan's bags.

"See?" I said.

"It was really her," confirmed Ava.

"Thanks," I said. I was so relieved to have a witness.

Mia's mouth was twisted in a wry smile. "I'm still not sure. It could have been anyone."

"So ask someone!" I said.

Katie looked around and spied an employee in a black Dylan's Candy Bar T-shirt.

"Excuse me," she said, walking over to him.

"But was that just Taylor Swift who was in here?"

The guy grinned. "Yes, it was!"

"Ha! See!" I crowed.

Katie smiled at him. "Thanks."

Mia grinned now too. "Wow! We saw Taylor Swift!"

"Humph. Some of us," I grumped.

"We *all* did," said Ava, glaring at me meaningfully. "Peacemaker." She wagged her finger at me and laughed.

"Pretty cool," I said, burning with happiness.

"No trip to New York is complete without a celebrity sighting," Katie said.

Mr. Cruz appeared with his arms laden with candy. "Who saw a celebrity?"

"Papi! We just saw Taylor Swift!" cried Mia.

"You did not! You can't pull that one on me. I wasn't born yesterday." He laughed.

"Oh boy, here we go again," I said.

"Papi, are you buying all that candy?" Mia asked sternly.

Mr. Cruz looked down at his armload and grinned in embarrassment. "I guess not," he said, and he gently unloaded it into a basket. *Sorry,* he mouthed at the salesguy.

"Ha-ha. Don't worry. This happens all the

time," the salesguy said with another chuckle.

As we walked out to catch a subway home, I said, "You know, I liked this place better than anything else."

"Even Omen?" cried Katie.

"Even Omen," I said solemnly.

CHAPTER 10

BFFs—Both Old and New

We were pooped by the time we got back to Mr. Cruz's apartment. I couldn't believe how much of the city we'd seen and also how little of the surface we'd scratched. We hadn't even hit any of the things on my own list, and I knew there were hundreds, maybe thousands, more fun things to do and see here.

Back at Mr. Cruz's we all flopped on the sofas in the living room to watch TV while he went out to hit the gym and work off all the cupcakes. Ava stayed for a little while, but then it was time for her to go to her ballet rehearsal. Her mom came to pick her up in their car downstairs.

Katie and I stood to hug her good-bye and make promises to see one another again soon.

"Take good care of Mia for me," cautioned Ava. "Katie, you're the boss when I'm not around. And, Alexis, keep up the good peacemaking."

I laughed. "Will do."

"And for goodness' sake, try to get into the city a little more often, please. Your urban education is really lacking, and I'm just the person to remedy that situation."

"Okay," I agreed. "But then you have to promise to come out to Maple Grove very soon. You can always stay with me if Mia's not being nice, you know."

"Me?!" cried Mia, all indignant now.

Katie rolled her eyes at me and laughed. "Why would you start all this up again, Alexis?"

"Kidding!" I said.

"Seriously, thanks, you two, for making me feel so included," said Ava. "I do sometimes get jealous and feel left out of Mia's new life and all her new friends."

"You aren't left out!" I said. "We're *your* new friends too!"

"Thanks," said Ava.

We gave Ava one more big hug good-bye and promised to Skype one day soon, and then Mia went with her downstairs to say hi to Ava's mom.

Katie and I re-flopped, and I asked if she'd mind if we changed the channel to *Celebrity Ballroom*, which she didn't. We watched for a while in silence as a minor Olympian and a former talk-show host did the tango. They were pretty great, actually, and when the host interviewed them after, little clips of the dance were replayed to illustrate what he was talking about.

"The best partners make their partner look great, am I right?" the host asked. He showed a clip of the male partner dipping the female, and she looked light as a feather, even though she was not a small person.

"Absolutely," agreed the woman. "Jerry made me feel like a princess, and he made it all look so effortless. He made me show my best self out there!"

"Well, that's just wonderful," gushed the host. Blah, blah, blah.

But the woman's words echoed in my head. It was like Madame Khalil. Like Dylan's Candy Bar. The best things in life take the basics and make them better. The best friends in life make you your best self. Funnier, a better baker, smarter, more graceful—whatever it is.

I turned to share this observation with Katie, but she had actually fallen asleep on the sofa, curled into a little ball. It was okay. The person I really wanted to share this idea with was Emma, who was due back at her house in Maple Grove tomorrow morning. I couldn't wait to see her back home and fill her in on everything we'd done. It wouldn't all seem real until the retelling. I would be careful to tell her repeatedly how much we missed her and how it wasn't the same without her and how we talked about her all the time. That was all true. But I wouldn't tell her what I was just realizing, deep down inside: that it had been good for me to branch out, to spend time with Mia and Katie (and Ava, of course) and get some new experience with other friends. I could now see I'd been relying on Emma too much, and it wasn't good for either of us. I needed to take the bull by the horns and make plans and put myself out there to enrich my life. It wouldn't diminish Emma's role at all; in fact, it might enhance it. Who knew?

Mia came back upstairs and saw Katie sleeping and gestured that she was going to go lie down in her room, too. It seemed like a great idea all around. For a minute I almost considered taking a train back alone tonight, just to sleep in my own bed and, to be perfectly honest, to be already in Maple Grove to see Emma. But I knew it could wait another day.

In fact, it should wait another day. I closed my eyes to rest them for just a minute, and I, of course, fell asleep too.

I woke up about an hour later to hear Mr. Cruz and Mia talking quietly in the kitchen. Katie stirred too, and we laughed at ourselves for not being able to hack the NYC pace without a nap.

Mia heard us, and she and her dad came in to chat and make a dinner plan.

"Do you guys want to go out or order in tonight?" Mia offered.

"What's on the agenda?" I asked.

"Well, we were planning to stay here until seven"—she and Katie exchanged a look that I didn't understand—"but then we had been thinking of going out for pizza at this brick-oven place by the guy who started the Sullivan Street Bakery."

"I could do that," I said, shrugging.

"Alexis, is there anything on *your* agenda?" asked Mr. Cruz with a smile. "We've certainly heard a lot about Mia and Katie's agenda this weekend."

I grinned. "Their agenda is my agenda. I am perfectly happy to leave all the planning to them. I organize us for business, they handle pleasure. But I'm learning, that's for sure."

"O-kaaaaay . . . ," said Mr. Cruz. "If you're sure?"

"I'm sure."

"If we ordered in instead of going out, what would we get?" asked Katie.

"Ooh, you've asked the million-dollar question around here." Mr. Cruz went to a cabinet and took out a big accordion folder. "There are many choices, my friends. Sometimes Mia and I are craving different things, so we order from different places. I'll have Chinese and she'll have a burrito. Or I'll get lobster and she'll have ribs. It just depends."

"Wow."

He opened the folder and showed us dozens and dozens of take-out menus from all different kinds of places.

"How can you ever decide?" I asked.

"Sometimes I just toss a few in the air and grab whichever one comes down first," he joked.

"Really?" asked Mia.

"No," he said, and he shook his head and laughed.

"I can't imagine living somewhere where you could get basically anything you can dream of delivered to your own front door. It's kind of wild! Maybe we should just order in pizza?" I suggested, which was my first suggestion of the trip.

"Yeah. And order up a movie?" Katie suggested.

"If you think that's good enough? I mean, we *are* in New York City!" said Mia.

I shrugged. "Sometimes the best kind of social plan is having no plan at all." But then I thought back to my empty days at home. "If it's by choice, that is. And only then."

At seven o'clock the doorbell rang, and Mia ran to get it. I didn't really stop to think that it was odd she'd be paying for the food, but when I heard laughter and squealing in the hall, I stood to go check on her. Where was Mr. Cruz? I wondered.

But out in the hall, I couldn't believe my eyes! It was Emma!

"Emma? Emma!" I cried, and I galloped over to grab her in a huge hug. "OMG, how did you get here?" I was so excited, I nearly cried, and I am not a big crier.

"Let the poor girl get in the door!" admonished Katie. "So I can say hi to her!" Katie gave Emma a big hug too, saying, "We missed you!"

"Thanks! I missed you guys, too!"

Emma dumped her stuff, and we all went into the living room to catch up. I was so, so happy, I couldn't stop smiling at Emma. Now the trip felt complete. I just knew I wouldn't have been able to savor the memories in the same way without her having been here too. I'd always be swallowing my comments, not wanting her to feel left out. Phew. This way was much better.

After explaining how Mia had had her dad text Emma's mom this morning to organize all this, Emma told us all about the camping trip and how there'd been a snake in the tent and the water was freezing, but also how they'd seen a rainbow and climbed a mountain to see the sunrise, and cooked fish they'd caught themselves. It sounded pretty great.

"Hey, maybe next year we could all go camping together," I suggested.

"Yeah!" Everyone liked that idea, and I think Emma was pleased her trip sounded so fun, we wanted to do it too.

"And next time we come here, Emma has to come for the whole time," said Mia. "Not just the very end."

"Thanks!" said Emma. "Hey, where's Ava?"

We explained where she was, and then we filled her in on everything we'd done, and it did really sound like a lot. It *had* been a lot.

"Aren't you guys exhausted?" Emma asked

incredulously, and we had to admit that we were.

"Not that we'll be low energy for you tonight!" Mia said with a grin.

"No, I myself am low energy." She giggled. "Sleeping on the ground doesn't do wonders for feeling rested."

"I call sleeping in a bed!" I joked, and Emma looked confused while the others laughed, so I had to explain it to her.

"Oh, you can totally have the bed, actually. An air mattress will feel like heaven to my achy bones right now."

"No, no. You take the bed. Please!" I insisted. "Especially for your achy bones."

"Well, we'll see," said Emma. "Thanks, though. What I really need is a professional massage with one of those rose oils my mom's always talking about."

"Oh, wait! That reminds me!" I ran into Mia's room and grabbed the little Soapy Chic bag. Returning to the living room, I reached into the bag and pulled out a bottle for each girl, checking the tag to be sure the right person had the right bottle.

They tore open the wrappings and said, "Yum!" Then they opened their bottles to use the cream.

"Oh, Alexis, these are awesome. You are so thoughtful. Thank you," said Mia.

"Yeah, I love mine. You're the best," Katie said.

"You're welcome," I said. "Sometimes a good idea strikes me and I plan ahead." And then we all laughed again, because I always plan ahead. At least when it comes to the important stuff.

Over pizza, we filled Emma in on all of our cupcake research: Georgetown, Billy's, Magnolia, and the Sprinkles cupcakes sold at Dylan's.

"By the way, the real money is in wholesaling," I said.

Emma looked at me blankly.

"I'll explain another time. But it's that or just selling cupcake mixes."

"Ew! I'd never use a mix!" said Katie.

"You'd be surprised," I said. "Lots of research goes into them."

"Wait, I thought you were going into the candy store business?" asked Mia.

"That too," I confessed. "Maybe I'll run Dylan's one day."

"I would not be surprised," teased Emma.

"Now, I hate to bring this up, but since we're all here . . ."

"The PTA." Mia moaned, putting her head in her hands.

"Right!" I said.

Katie sighed. "You know where I stand. I think we should just make the best possible plain vanilla and plain chocolate cupcakes, with alternate icing, and call it a day. If we can do simple perfectly, scrumptiously, then they'll know we can be trusted with anything."

"I kind of agree," said Mia. "I think we could do plain cake and frosting, but decorate them really wildly, like with candy from Dylan's or fondant flowers, or use wild cupcake wrappers, and sprinkles—whatever."

"But we don't want them to look junky or unappetizing . . . ," complained Katie.

"Hold on!" I said while putting my palms out peacemaker-style. "We're just in the brainstorming mode. Emma?"

"I think we should do one totally wild and one totally simple, to show our range."

"Okay, and I think we should just blow it out. I mean, do our most unique stuff. Everyone knows we can do plain and basic. Why not showcase what we're capable of?"

We all sat in silence, chewing.

Mr. Cruz spoke up. We'd all kind of forgotten he was there again.

"Can I put in my two cents?"

"Sure, Papi," said Mia.

"I think you're all right. So why don't you put all the possibilities into a hat and pick three?"

We were quiet for a second, and then we all broke into smiles. "Great idea," I said.

"Thanks. Sometimes I have them," Mr. Cruz said smugly.

"Sometimes," teased Mia.

And so that is how, one week later, we ended up at the PTA meeting with three platters of cupcakes. One was kind of our trademark: salted caramel cupcakes with bacon frosting. Another was our Mud Pies, something we'd made once for Jake Taylor's birthday party. It was chocolate cake with chocolate frosting and with chunks of Oreo cookies and chocolate chips stuck in the frosting. And the final ones were our minis that we make for our friend Mona, who owns The Special Day bridal salon in the mall in Maple Grove. They were vanilla cake with vanilla frosting, about the size of a fifty-cent piece: tiny and delicious.

See if you can guess which ones went the fastest?

Yup.

The vanilla-vanilla minis.

And the bacon? About half got eaten.

The Mud Pies? Barely at all. (I hate wasting cupcakes; it's money out of our pockets, even though the Taylor boys are always glad to take extra inventory off our hands.)

When we picked up our trays and leftovers after the meeting, we analyzed the results.

"Well, grown-ups—all the moms especially—are always trying to eat healthy or lose weight or whatever, so it's no surprise they went for the minis."

"Plus, vanilla appeals to everyone. Surprisingly, chocolate doesn't," said Katie.

"Yeah, I think all the bacon ones were eaten by dads," said Emma. "I know those are my older brothers' favorite."

"But, hey, we did hand out a ton of flyers and business cards," said Katie. "Alexis, you've got to be pleased by that!"

I nodded, and then I tried to sum it all up for us, to make it into a learning experience. "So all cupcakes are good, in different combinations. But the simpler, the better."

Mia squinted. "Kind of like friends," she said.

I laughed.

"Yeah. And plans," Emma added.

"And clothes?" suggested Katie.

"And candy!" I said.

We all laughed then.

"Hey, look, guys! It's Taylor Swift!"

We all laughed again and ended in a big group hug before we took our leftovers and went home in good old Maple Grove. It felt great to have the four of us together, in any and all combinations. I was glad there was school the next day (I know, I know) and I could get back into my routine with my friends. I was glad I had branched out and tried new things, and I knew I'd try to do more of it, but sometimes you just need things to be easy and peaceful. And speaking of peace, I, for one, had lots of *Celebrity Ballroom* to watch.

Want another sweet cupcake?
Here's a sneak peek
of the seventeenth book in the

CUPCAKE DIARIES

series:

Katie
sprinkles & surprises

Mia, My Personal Adviser

$\mathcal{M}$ake them stop!" I cried, laughing. "They're tickling my nose! I'm going to sneeze!"

But my best friend, Mia, can be a little harsh sometimes. "But they *like* you!" she protested, doubled over giggling.

I was sleeping over at Mia's house, and even though she has a perfectly comfortable brand-new bed, she spread out her sleeping bag on the floor next to mine, so we could hang out and talk. But whenever anyone lies on the floor, Mia's little fluffy dogs, Tiki and Milkshake, think that it's playtime. So both of them were dancing around my face, sniffing me and licking my nose.

"Seriously, Mia!" I pleaded. "Call off your ferocious beasts!"

"Okay! Okay!" Mia got up and scooped up one wriggling dog in each arm. "Sorry, babies. Katie doesn't want to play with you."

She dropped them out the door and then shut it quickly.

"I like playing with them," I said, sitting up. "But they were attacking me."

"Those two? They're afraid of ants," Mia joked.

"They're terrors," I said. "But at least they're cute. It's too bad Mom is allergic to pets. I would love to have a dog. A big fluffy one."

Then there was a knock on the door.

"Girls, it's ice-cream time," announced Mia's stepdad, Eddie.

I smiled. "That's my favorite time of day!"

We both jumped up and followed Eddie down the stairs to the kitchen, where the table was set up for an ice-cream sundae buffet. There were three cartons of ice cream, a bottle of chocolate sauce, a can of whipped cream, and bowls filled with cherries, sprinkles, and crumbled-up cookies.

Mia's stepbrother, Dan, was leaning against the kitchen sink, eating out of a bowl that looked like it was mostly filled with whipped cream.

"What are you guys, twins?" he asked. (I forgot to mention that Dan is in high school. I have come to believe that most high school boys are kind of rude—that's just how they are. Well, except for my friend Emma's brother Sam. He is perfect.)

Anyway, I should explain why Dan made that crack about us being twins. It's because Mia and I were wearing matching pajamas, pink ones with a cupcake pattern on them. We had bought them with the money we had made from the cupcake business we're in with our friends Emma and Alexis. It's kind of funny. Any time I make money from the cupcakes, I end up spending it on something cupcake related. Last time, I got this cool stenciling kit you can use to make designs on your cupcakes. I guess you can say I am cupcake obsessed.

Mia is not as cupcake obsessed as I am, but she loved the pajamas as much as I did. And the sleepover was the perfect time to wear them.

"Yes, we're twins," Mia replied to Dan sarcastically, because apparently the best way to deal with a rude teenage boy is to be rude back. It must have worked, because Dan just shrugged and kept eating.

Eddie was anxious for us to dig in. "Come on, girls. The combination possibilities are endless!"

Mia's mom, Mrs. Valdes, entered the kitchen and gave Eddie a hug. "What a sweet thing to do, honey," she said. "Thanks!"

Mia looked at me and rolled her eyes again. I know it makes her all cringey when her mom and stepdad get lovey-dovey in front of her.

"Yes, thanks, Mr. Valdes," I said. "This looks amazing."

"What are you waiting for? Dig in before it melts!" Eddie said, motioning to us.

Mia grabbed a bowl and spoon and then stood there, thinking. I knew whatever she made would not only be the perfect balance of flavor, but also beautiful. Mia is a true artist. I'm not so picky. I took my bowl and started piling in everything.

Chocolate, mint chip, and butter pecan ice cream. Chocolate syrup, cookie crumbles, and cherries. Then I sprayed on the whipped cream and finally added the sprinkles.

"Katie, those sprinkles are going to fall off," Mia remarked.

"You have to put them on last," I informed her. "Because they make it pretty."

Rainbow sprinkles are my favorite, because they're so colorful. Sometimes when people ask me what my favorite color is, I say "rainbow" because I just can't decide. Mom heard me say it so much that she got me rainbow socks for Christmas. They're my favorite.

I sat down at the table and was already halfway done eating my ice cream when Mia finally finished creating her bowl. As I predicted, it was a work of art. Mia had a perfect scoop of chocolate ice cream in her bowl, topped by a flower design painted with chocolate syrup. The center of the flower was a cherry.

"Mia, that's gorgeous!" I said.

Mia grinned. "And delicious!" Then she dug in her spoon.

I gave a mock scream. "Aah! You've destroyed your art!"

"It's for a good cause," Mia said, eating another spoonful.

When we finished we helped to clean up the kitchen and then went back up to Mia's room and sprawled out on the floor again, this time without dogs.

"I'm so glad you could sleep over tonight!" Mia said. "What's your mom doing again?"

"She and her new boyfriend are going to see a Broadway show, and she won't be back till late," I said. "She figured it would be better if I slept over than if she came and got me at midnight."

"That's good, but we'll still be awake at midnight," Mia said. "Remember last time? We were up until three! That was so much fun!"

I nodded. "And then Eddie made us pancakes at, like, the crack of dawn. I was so tired!"

Then I paused. There was something I had been wanting to ask Mia.

"So, Mia, I need your advice," I began. "Of all my friends, you are the best expert on this topic."

"What topic?" Mia asked.

"Moms with boyfriends," I said. "I mean, your mom and Eddie dated for a while before they got married, right?"

Mia nodded. "Yeah."

"Was Eddie always so nice?" I asked. "For a stepdad, he seems really great."

"He is," Mia said. "But it was still weird when they started dating. I kind of kept hoping that Mom would get back together with my dad, you know?"

I nodded, but I really didn't know. Mia's mom and dad got divorced just a few years ago, but my dad left me and my mom when I was a little baby. I didn't grow up with him or anything. So there isn't any part of me that wants to see them get back together. But I could understand why Mia might feel that way.

"So, why are you asking?" Mia asked. "Because of this new boyfriend?"

"Jeff," I replied. "I haven't met him yet. All I know about him is that he's a teacher or something, which isn't too exciting, if you ask me. And he likes to run, and he has a daughter who's younger than I am."

"Does your mom like him?" Mia asked.

"A lot, I think," I told her. "She's, like, happy all the time. She doesn't get mad anymore when I do dumb stuff, like leave my socks on the floor."

"Hmm," Mia said thoughtfully. "Mom was like that right before she and Eddie got serious."

"That's what I'm afraid of," I said. "On the drive over here she said it's time for me to meet Jeff. Like, in person!"

"How else would you meet him?" Mia asked.

"You know what I mean," I said. "Until now, he's been more of . . . an idea. But once I meet him, it will all be real."

Mia looked thoughtful. "You know, Eddie was the only boyfriend Mom ever introduced me to. I think she waited until she knew she was serious about him."

"But what about your dad?" Katie asked. "Is he serious about Lynn?"

I knew Mia's dad had been dating a woman named Lynn, who had a little boy who was kind of a pain. And Mia had gotten stuck "entertaining" him a lot.

"I think dads are different," Mia answered. "He's introduced me to other girlfriends before Lynn, and they didn't last. So Lynn might not last either."

"So maybe Jeff won't last?" I asked a little bit hopefully.

But Mia shook her head. "No, I'm pretty sure when moms do it, they mean it."

I groaned. "I thought so. I hope he's as nice as Eddie."

"I hope so too," Mia said. "But look on the bright side. You have the upper hand here. If you hate him, your mom is going to have a problem. If he hates you, it's his problem."

"I don't know," I said. "I'm still nervous."

Mia flopped over onto her back. "It'll work out," she said. "So, hey, did you hear about the new math teacher?"

"Oh yeah!" I replied, quickly forgetting all about the Jeff problem. "Mr. Green, right? Everyone keeps talking about how cool he is."

"He replaced Mr. Rodriguez," Mia reported. "Mr. Rodriguez left town because his wife got a great new job in Chicago. So now Emma has Mr. Green. She says he's really funny and sweet.

And I heard that at his old school, he got elected Teacher of the Year, like, five times in a row."

"Wow," I said. "Is he going to coach boys' track, too, like Mr. Rodriguez did?"

Mia nodded. "He just started. And you know what? I've heard a bunch of girls showed up to his first track practice just so they could stare at him."

"Gross! He's a teacher!" I said, making a face.

"And guess what else I heard?" Mia asked. "Olivia Allen has the biggest crush in the world on him. She's in the same class as Emma, and Emma says Olivia even goes to get extra after-school help from him even though she's pretty good at math. She's just faking it."

I shook my head. "That is so weird, but it's exactly something Olivia would do!"

Mia and I gossiped some more, and even though we stayed up late, we fell asleep just before midnight. That night I dreamed Mom took me into this white room with a door, and she said, "Katie, I'd like you to meet Jeff." And then she opened the door, and do you know what was behind it?

An ice-cream sundae with sprinkles! That's what I get for eating ice cream late at night.

"Nice to Meet You" Cupcakes

After talking to Mia I felt a lot better about the idea of meeting Jeff in person. I was banking on the fact that if I liked him, everything would be cool, and if I didn't like him, Mom would probably dump him.

But I still wasn't prepared the next day when Mom told me she had actually set up a time for me and Jeff to meet. She broke the news on Sunday night, when we were eating Chinese food on the couch and watching shows on the food channel together.

"So," Mom said, during a commercial. "I've invited Jeff over for dinner Saturday night."

"What?" I asked, letting a forkful of cold sesame noodles fall right onto my lap.

"Like we talked about," Mom said.

"I know," I said. "It's just I didn't think it would be so soon."

Mom looked concerned. She has brown eyes like I do, and they're very expressive. It's easy to tell when she's worried or sad. "Do you really think it's too soon? Because I could cancel."

Right then I had a tough decision to make. All I had to do was say so and Mom would call it off. But I kind of felt bad for Mom. I know she really likes Jeff. And, I mean, she hasn't had a serious boyfriend for, like, ever.

I sighed. "Saturday is okay."

Mom put her right arm across my shoulders and gave me a squeeze. "Thank you, Katie. I know you'll like him."

I didn't say anything, and the show came back on. I finished my sesame noodles and then cracked open a fortune cookie.

"*Good things come to those who wait,*" read the fortune inside.

I looked at Mom. Was this fortune for her? I slipped the fortune into the pocket of my pajama pants.

The next day at school I decided it was time to give all my friends the Jeff details.

"So, my mom is inviting her boyfriend over for dinner Saturday night so I can meet him," I blurted out at the lunch table. Sometimes it's just easier to tell people stuff that way.

"You mean Jeff?" Emma asked. She's a good listener; she always remembers every detail of every story you tell her.

I nodded. "Yeah, I might as well get it over with. But Mia made me feel better. I figure if I don't like him, Mom will break up with him."

Emma frowned. "Maybe. But didn't you see that movie on the romance network? This girl's mom had a boyfriend, and the girl didn't like him, but the mom married him, anyway, and it turned out he was a secret jewel thief."

I suddenly felt worried. "I didn't see it, but it was based on a true story, right?"

Alexis interjected. "Katie, your mom is a lot smarter than that woman in the movie. If she thinks he's a nice, good guy, then you'll probably like him too. Besides, it's just one dinner. You can't let too much ride on it."

"Alexis is right, Katie. That woman in the movie was nothing like your mom," Emma agreed.

"Katie's mom is so nice," Mia remarked.

"Definitely," Emma said. Then her blue eyes

got big. "Oh, I know. At our cupcake meeting on Thursday we should bake cupcakes for the dinner!"

"You mean, like, 'Hey Jeff, I hope you're not a creep' cupcakes?" I asked.

"More like 'Nice to meet you' cupcakes," Emma said, laughing.

"It's a good idea," Alexis said. "We have a request for strawberry cupcakes for a party in a few weeks. We can test out the recipe."

"Wait? So now Jeff is a cupcake guinea pig?" I asked. "What happened to 'nice to meet you'?"

"He won't know the difference," Alexis pointed out. "Besides, it's the thought that counts."

"Sounds good," I said. "Text me the recipe, so I can make sure we have the ingredients."

I heard my cell phone beep in my backpack ten seconds later. Alexis is superorganized. That night Mom and I went shopping for the ingredients, and on Thursday we were ready for our cupcake meeting.

The Cupcake Club meets every Friday during school lunch, but we have to meet at other times too because business has been pretty good since we started. Alexis handles most of the business stuff, because she's best at it. She keeps track of how much money we earn and spend and keeps a record of our supplies and other expenses. She also makes sure our clients pay us, which is important.

Some meetings, all we do is business stuff, which is boring but important. At other meetings, we bake cupcakes for our clients or test out new cupcake recipes. It's important to try new flavors, because if you don't test them, then you won't know if they're good or not until it's too late, and all it takes is one bad batch of cupcakes for a client to ruin our business. That's why it was a good idea for us to make a batch of the strawberry cupcakes that day. And yeah, they have a mix for that, but we make our cupcakes from scratch. "From scratch" means we make everything fresh, from the beginning. That's why they're so good!

Alexis, Emma, and Mia all got to my house at five. My mom had started a batch of veggie chili in the Crock-Pot that morning, so we could all eat dinner after our meeting. We got started baking right away. My friends and I have gotten pretty good at baking together. Usually two of us work on the batter while the other two do the icing. Alexis knew the strawberry cake recipe by heart from studying it, so she and I did the batter together.

"It's not easy to get cake to taste like strawberry without using artificial flavor," Alexis remarked.

"But I think the jam in this batter is going to be nice."

"And using homemade strawberry syrup to flavor the icing will really taste good," I added.

Mia was stirring the mix of strawberries, water, and sugar on top of the stove while my mom looked on.

"It smells awesome," Mia reported.

The strawberry syrup cooled while we baked the cupcakes in the oven. Then Mia and Emma mixed the syrup in the blender with butter and powdered sugar to make the frosting. When the cupcakes were done, we had to wait for them to cool before we iced them, so Mom spooned us bowls of veggie chili. Mia and I put sliced jalapeños on top of ours, because we like things spicy. After the chili, we iced the cupcakes.

"They look so pretty," Emma said admiringly.

"The client wants pink flowers on top, but you can work on that, right, Mia?" Alexis asked.

Mia nodded. "No problem." She designs most of our cupcake decorations.

"These look great, but they're kind of boring for 'nice to meet you' cupcakes," I said.

Mom's face perked up. "Oh? Who are these for?"

"We thought we could use some for our dinner

with Jeff," I said, and Mom looked like she might burst with happiness.

"Oh, that's so sweet of all of you," she said, beaming. "Thank you! He will love them."

"I hope he likes pink," Alexis said.

"If he doesn't like pink, then he's just not a good boyfriend," I announced, which made no sense at all if you think about it. But Mom didn't look worried. "Anyway, I still think they look boring."

Then I remembered the sleepover with Mia and had an idea. I ran into the kitchen closet and came out with a container of rainbow sprinkles.

"These make everything better," I said with a grin, and I grabbed a spoon and started sprinkling the cupcakes.

Alexis shook her head. "You are rainbow crazy."

"Sprinkles are great," Mia said. "They cover up any mess you make with the icing."

"And they're pretty besides!" I added.

When we were done, we had a plate of very cheerful cupcakes. We stood back and admired our work.

"If Jeff doesn't like these, then he has no soul!" I said.

Want more

CUPCAKE DIARIES?

Visit **CupcakeDiariesBooks.com**
for the series trailer, excerpts, activities,
and everything you need for throwing
your own cupcake party!

The Missing Ingredients

"Boy did I mess up this time," Alexis said. Right away the rest of the Cupcake Club turned to look at her. "Oh great, and we're already late—this is really going to throw us off schedule."

"Why, did we do something wrong?" Emma asked.

"No, it's not you," Alexis said with a sigh. "See this shopping list? Useless! Give me your phone."

As Emma passed Alexis her phone, Mia and Katie wondered what was wrong.

"Really, Alexis, it can't be that bad, can it?" Katie asked. Alexis didn't answer.

"Now what?" Mia wondered aloud as Alexis shouted into the phone.

"Dylan, you left the most important ingredients off our shopping list for our famous brown sugar and bacon cupcakes, and now we have to go back to the store. *Bye!*" Alexis took a deep breath and handed the phone back to Emma. "Can't have a boy-crazy girl write out your shopping list," she said. "Oh well. Next time I'll know better, but right now we have to get back to the store—and fast!"

What ingredients did Dylan leave off the shopping list?

Circle the first letter of each sentence, and write it below on the lines. (If you don't want to write in your book, make a copy of this page.)

__ __ __ __ __   __ __ __ __ __ __   __ __ __   __ __ __ __ __!

What Are Your Plans?

"Failing to plan is planning to fail," is one of Alexis's mottos. As you read in this story, Alexis writes down everything she plans to do—even if it's something silly like "Eat churros!"

Here's your chance to be like Alexis for a day. Make a plan for Saturday. Then put this page in a safe place so you won't lose it. (Don't forget to write down to "Have fun!")

(If you don't want to write in your book, make a copy of these pages.)

DATE: _____

TIME I PLAN TO WAKE UP: _____

WHAT I PLAN TO EAT FOR BREAKFAST: _____

_____

WHAT I NEED TO DO AFTER BREAKFAST:

_____

_____

WHAT I *WANT* TO DO AFTER BREAKFAST:

_____

_____

WHO I WANT TO CALL:

_____

WHAT I PLAN TO EAT FOR LUNCH:

_____

WHAT I PLAN TO DO IN THE AFTERNOON:

_____

_____

WHAT I PLAN TO EAT FOR DINNER:

YUM!

_____

WHAT I PLAN TO DO SATURDAY NIGHT:

_____

_____

ANSWER KEY

The Missing Ingredients

What ingredients did Dylan leave off the shopping list?

BROWN SUGAR AND BACON!

Coco Simon always dreamed of opening a cupcake bakery but was afraid she would eat all of the profits. When she's not daydreaming about cupcakes, Coco edits children's books and has written close to one hundred books for children, tweens, and young adults, which is a lot less than the number of cupcakes she's eaten. Cupcake Diaries is the first time Coco has mixed her love of cupcakes with writing.

You're never too young to change the world!

These second graders in North Carolina fundraised to sponsor one year of school for Jarana in Nepal

They're changing the world. You can too with:

GOAL Getters!

With **GOAL Getters** in the classroom, you will:

* Learn how to be a leader in your community
* Host creative fundraisers like bake sales!
* Give girls the opportunity to go to school!

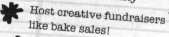

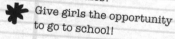

Talk to your teacher and visit
shesthefirst.org/GOALGetters

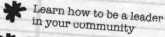

GOAL Getters
Global Opportunities, Awareness, Leadership

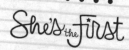

She's the First

Still Hungry?
There's always room for another Cupcake!

Katie and the
Cupcake Cure

1

Mia in the Mix

2

Emma on Thin Icing

3

Alexis and the
Perfect Recipe

4

Katie, Batter Up!

5

Mia's Baker's Dozen

6

Emma All Stirred Up!

7

Alexis
Cool as a Cupcake

8

Katie and the
Cupcake War
9

Mia's Boiling Point
10

Emma, Smile and
Say "Cupcake!"
11

Alexis Gets Frosted
12

Katie's New Recipe
13

Mia
a Matter of Taste
14

Emma Sugar and Spice
and Everything Nice
15

Alexis and the
Missing Ingredient
16

Katie
Sprinkles & Surprises
17

Chatham County Libraries
500 N. 2nd Avenue
Siler City, North Carolina 27344